His kiss

For a moment, nothing else mattered except the wild, sweet longing that surged through Maddie's veins.

"Madeleine," Colton rasped, "I don't think…"

"Shh." She bent down to brush a searing kiss over his lips, and then lingered for several long, tantalizing seconds. She couldn't help herself. The taste of him, the feel of him, was irresistible. Then, before he could guess her intent, she pushed his hand over his head and quickly snapped on the other handcuff.

"What the…?" He twisted his head and stared in bemusement at his shackled wrists.

He fixed her with a hard glare, his dark eyes beginning to focus with awareness of what she was doing. "Don't do this, Madeleine." His voice sounded rough, still groggy with sleep. "Uncuff me right this damned minute."

Maddie bit her lip. Colton gave a roar and bucked his hips in an attempt to unseat her. With a cry of alarm, Maddie found herself pitched onto the floor.

"It's no use, Colton," she gasped, and opened her hand to reveal the set of keys. "I already have them." Maddie pushed herself to her feet, intent only on grabbing her shoes and getting out of there.

"Madeleine," _____rs, "you can't run for _____ u to hide.

"I'll get free, _____…"

Dear Reader,

Growing up in the Boston area, I was familiar with the story of the MIT and Harvard University students who formed blackjack teams and used card-counting techniques to beat casinos at blackjack. But when my young nephew admitted that he had a knack for cards, and that he earned more money through gambling than he ever did through his summer jobs, I was both intrigued and alarmed.

This was the genesis of Maddie's story, a woman who learns her younger brother—the only family member she has left—is not only caught up in gambling, but has gotten himself into trouble with some truly dangerous men. Desperate times call for desperate measures, and in an effort to help her brother, Maddie soon finds herself on the wrong side of the law. Good thing for her, she has U.S. deputy marshal Colton Black hot on her trail, and if there's one thing he's good at, it's always getting his man—or woman!

I hope you enjoy Maddie and Colton's story, and that you'll look for U.S. marshal Jason Cooper's story, coming in April!

Happy reading!

Karen

1

UNDER NORMAL CIRCUMSTANCES, Colton Black wouldn't have given the girl a second glance. Tomboys weren't his type, and with her oversize T-shirt, baseball cap and backpack, there wasn't much of her to see anyway. Only the long, honeyed swish of a ponytail poking through the back of the cap, and a sweetly curved ass beneath a pair of faded blue jeans gave any hint of femininity. But it was neither of these that had captured Colton's attention.

Nope, it was definitely the gun.

Colton had barely glanced up from his breakfast when the big Greyhound bus pulled into the gravel parking lot of the diner located on a remote stretch of Interstate 80 in Lovelock, Nevada. Several travelers disembarked, either to refresh themselves before climbing back onto the bus, or to wait for a connecting one. There was a frazzled mother dragging a small, wailing boy in her wake, an elderly couple and the young woman in the baseball cap.

As they entered the diner, Colton had returned his

attention to his newspaper and finished eating. Afterward, he wasn't certain what had made him look up again. The girl had paused near the cash register, presumably to check out the array of gum and mints on display there, but the uncanny sixth sense that had saved his hide on numerous occasions was kicking into full gear, demanding his attention.

As he watched, the girl's hand fluttered to the waistband of her jeans beneath the T-shirt. Colton's eyes narrowed as she touched something hidden there. She hesitated, then dropped her arm back to her side, but not before he saw the dull, metallic glint of the weapon concealed beneath the shirt.

She turned toward the cashier, hesitated again, then seemed to change her mind. She moved slightly away, pretending to look at a rack of magazines. As Colton watched, she drew in a deep breath, as if bracing herself, before she turned resolutely back to the cashier. Colton was halfway to his feet when she made a jerky movement and spun abruptly on her heel. She ducked her head and strode past his booth to the rear of the diner, muttering something beneath her breath that sounded suspiciously like "Stupid, stupid, stupid!"

Colton reached into his wallet and tossed several bills onto the table. Cautiously, he made his way toward the back of the small restaurant, where the girl had disappeared. There was a tiny alcove with a public telephone, next to a door that led to the diner's single unisex bathroom, currently occupied by the mother and her small son; Colton could hear the boy still crying plaintively from behind the closed door.

Hard to Hold

—

Karen Foley

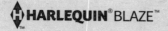

HARLEQUIN® BLAZE™

Recycling programs
for this product may
not exist in your area.

ISBN-13: 978-0-373-79790-5

HARD TO HOLD

HARLEQUIN®
www.Harlequin.com

Printed in U.S.A.

ABOUT THE AUTHOR

Karen Foley is an incurable romantic. When she's not working for the Department of Defense, she's writing sexy romances with strong heroes and happy endings. She lives in Massachusetts with her husband and two daughters, an overgrown puppy and two very spoiled cats. Karen enjoys hearing from her readers. You can find out more about her by visiting www.karenefoley.com.

Books by Karen Foley

HARLEQUIN BLAZE

353—FLYBOY
422—OVERNIGHT SENSATION
451—ABLE-BODIED
504—HOLD ON TO THE NIGHTS
549—BORN ON THE 4TH OF JULY
    "Packing Heat"
563—HOT-BLOODED
596—HEAT OF THE MOMENT
640—DEVIL IN DRESS BLUES
682—COMING UP FOR AIR
711—BLAZING BEDTIME STORIES, VOLUME IX
    "God's Gift to Women"
721—A KISS IN THE DARK
757—FREE FALL
776—A SOLDIER'S CHRISTMAS
    "If Only in My Dreams"

To get the inside scoop on Harlequin Blaze and its talented writers, be sure to check out blazeauthors.com.

All backlist available in ebook format. Don't miss any of our special offers. Write to us at the following address for information on our newest releases.

Harlequin Reader Service
U.S.: 3010 Walden Ave., P.O. Box 1325, Buffalo, NY 14269
Canadian: P.O. Box 609, Fort Erie, Ont. L2A 5X3

He leaned negligently against the wall as if waiting his turn for the restroom, but he needn't have bothered with the pretense. The girl was completely oblivious to his presence. She stood with her back to him, caught up in rehearsing what sounded suspiciously like a scene from the movie *Thelma and Louise.*

As Colton watched, she rolled her shoulders, assumed a cocky stance and then started again from the top in a low, husky voice. "All right, ladies and gentlemen, let's see who'll win the prize for keepin' their cool. Simon says everybody lie down on the floor. If nobody loses their head, then nobody loses their head." In the next instant, she gave an audible groan and her shoulders sagged. "I can't do this."

"Well, that's a relief," Colton drawled, startling her. "Because as of oh-five-hundred this morning, I'm on vacation, and I'd sure as hell hate to see it ruined on account of some dumb-ass kid looking to make a quick buck on the wrong side of the law."

At the sound of his voice, the girl whirled around with a sharp cry of surprise. Now she fumbled beneath her shirt and yanked the weapon free with jerky movements. Her hands were unsteady, but she was close enough that if she decided to pull the trigger, she wouldn't miss. Colton went still and raised his hands to show her he meant no harm, but he didn't retreat.

"Stop right there." Her voice was low and strained. "Take another step and I'll be forced to shoot."

Colton kept his eyes on her face, deliberately not looking at the weapon, but he'd already taken note of her stance. She had both hands clutched around the gun, aimed at his midsection, and it looked to him as if the safety lever was in the locked position. In the time it would take her to release the lever, he could easily take the gun from her. There'd be no contest.

He glanced at the patrons in the diner. The elderly couple who had come in on the Greyhound were seated at a booth as the waitress, a tired-looking woman in her fifties, scratched their order on a small pad of paper. The only other patron was an old man seated at the counter, his grizzled head bobbing lightly over his coffee cup.

Colton sighed. It was time to end this. If he did it right, nobody in the diner would be any wiser as to what was transpiring just behind them. The girl wouldn't even realize she'd been overpowered until it was too late. He'd just remove the gun from her hands, spin her around, push her up against the wall and contact the local authorities. And maybe, just maybe, he could still make it to his cabin before nightfall.

Then the girl tipped her head back, and muted light from the dust-covered windows spilled across her features. Colton found himself staring into hazel eyes the color of aged whiskey, fringed by lashes that were incongruously dark by comparison.

Not a girl. A woman.

He guessed her to be in her mid- to late twenties. Her oval face had a delicate bone structure, with high cheekbones and a slim, straight nose. The cleft in her chin suggested a strength or stubbornness that was completely belied by the soft fullness of her lips. But it was her eyes that had him raising his hands in a mute gesture of surrender.

The woman was terrified.

And desperate.

Colton had seen that look just twice before. Once, when he'd cornered a small fox that had found its way into his cabin. He'd thought the animal was going to either attack him outright or die of heart failure while he tried to figure out how to get it outside. In the end, he'd stepped aside, opened the screen door and watched as it bolted for freedom.

The second time...well, he just wished his choices then had been as easy as they'd been with the fox. Reluctantly, he recalled the incident at the San Diego federal courthouse six years earlier. A boy of about sixteen entered the courthouse, but as he had passed through the metal detectors, he'd had tripped the security alarm. Colton had been standing guard outside one of the courtrooms, assigned to protect the man on trial behind the closed doors. There had been no doubt that the defendant was complete scum, accused of aggravated kidnapping, rape and murder, but he was under federal protection. Colton was a Deputy U.S. Marshal; his job was to ensure the accused had his day in court.

As the alarm had sounded and the guards had moved forward to detain the boy, he'd broken free and bolted down the corridor, his youthful features twisted in anguish and a kind of fierce determination. Colton thought he'd always remember the sound of the kid's sneakers squeaking against the polished marble floors of the cavernous lobby. He had stepped forward to block him, his weapon drawn. The youth had slid to a stop, arms flung out for balance. When he saw the two guards advancing on him, he'd reached into his denim jacket and pulled out a gun.

The utter despair on his face as he'd weighed his options had caused Colton to hesitate for one fateful second. He'd cried out in denial even as he lunged forward to stay the boy's hand.

But he'd been too late.

The youth had put the gun to his own head, and the sound of a single shot reverberated through the lofty halls. His body had hit the floor before the last echoes faded. Later, Colton learned the boy had intended to kill the defendant he was protecting; the same man who had allegedly kidnapped, raped and then murdered the boy's young girlfriend.

Now Colton could see the same fleeting expressions of despair and steely resolve on this young woman's face as she stood facing him. She compressed her lips and steadied the gun, aimed now at his heart.

"Easy there," he heard himself say. "Why don't you put away the gun? I'm sure there's another way. You don't really want to do this."

Her eyes clung to his for a brief moment before shifting to the parking lot beyond the diner windows.

"Is one of those vehicles yours?"

Colton followed her gaze, sensing the direction of her thoughts. "Yes, ma'am."

Goddamn it to hell. His boss would have his head and maybe even his badge, but suddenly Colton didn't have a choice. Whatever trouble she was in, instinct told him that arresting her wasn't the solution, and could even be the one thing that drove her completely over the edge. He'd be damned if he'd have her on his conscience.

She gestured toward the door with her gun, and it was then that Colton realized he'd been duped. As she waved the weapon, his eyes were drawn to a scratch on the end of the barrel, revealing the bright orange plastic beneath. Only toy guns were equipped with brightly colored tips, as a way to prevent them from being mistaken for the real McCoy. Clearly, the tip of this one had been painted to match the barrel. As toy guns went, it was a damned realistic replica of the real thing.

"Good," the woman was saying. "I need you to drive me somewhere." She tipped her chin up, her eyes narrowing. "And don't try anything foolish, or I might have to use this. I—I'm a good shot, too."

Colton kept his face neutral. "I'm sure you are, ma'am."

He was frankly surprised at how far she was willing to play out this little drama. He'd seen a lot of bizarre and even twisted things in his eleven years as a Deputy U.S. Marshal, but he'd never encountered a situation quite like this one. He knew what he should do, but somehow the idea of exerting his authority over this woman, and destroying whatever small hope she had of getting out of this predicament, held little appeal for him. For now, at least, he'd play it out with her and go along as her "hostage." At least he could ensure she didn't try a similar stunt on some other unsuspecting person. Hell, she could find herself at the wrong end of a shotgun, especially in these rural areas where most business owners kept a loaded weapon behind the counter as a matter of course.

Eventually, he'd have to let her know the game was up. But for the moment, he was intrigued enough to find out what her motives were, what kind of trouble she was in and just how far she might be willing to go. He'd been hoping to make it to his cabin by dinner, but decided his vacation could wait another hour or so.

Concealing the weapon beneath her shirt, the woman stepped behind him, indicating he should precede her out of the diner. "Just walk a little in front of me, okay? Don't turn around. If you do, I'll have no choice but to use the gun. Are we clear?"

Colton's lips twitched, but he nodded solemnly. "Yes, ma'am."

They'd just reached the diner's entrance when the door to the bathrooms opened, and Colton could hear the frazzled mother and her young son, who was still wailing.

"Whatever you left on the bus will still be there when we get back on," the mom was saying, trying to console the boy.

Colton found himself suddenly propelled through the door as his "captor" crowded against him, pushing the gun into the middle of his back. "Hurry." Her voice was low and urgent.

Colton obliged, moving through the door and into the suffocating heat of the sun-baked parking lot. But as the door swung shut behind him, he could just make out the child's reply.

"But, Mommy, I left my *gun* on the seat! What if someone takes it?"

Then the door closed and it was just the two of them. Colton barely contained his snort of disbelief. He wondered how she'd react if he reached out and yanked the useless weapon from under her shirt.

The woman was looking sharply at him. Colton knew she was trying to determine if he'd heard the boy, and if he had, whether or not he'd made the connection between the child's toy and her weapon.

He kept his face carefully impassive and continued across the dusty parking lot. She hesitated for a moment and Colton glanced back at her. He knew in that moment that she had, indeed, taken the child's toy from where he had left it on the bus. The combination of guilt and consternation on her face had Colton wondering if she might not march back into the diner and return it to the child. Just when he was certain she was going to do exactly that, she composed her features into a mask of steely resolve, and the moment passed.

"Which of these is yours?" She nodded toward the parked vehicles.

"The pickup there." Colton indicated a black truck that dominated the lot. A canvas tarp was stretched across the bed, protecting and concealing the provisions and gear he was bringing with him to the cabin for a two-week fishing vacation.

"Okay, you drive." The woman stood aside as he unlocked the vehicle. "Wait!"

Colton stopped just as he was preparing to climb behind the wheel, and turned to look at her expectantly. Her brow was furrowed.

"This isn't right," she muttered.

"Nope," Colton agreed, "it ain't. Whatever your problem is, it can't be worth the pile of trouble you're getting yourself into by taking me hostage."

The woman waved her hand dismissively. "No, no. I mean *this* isn't right." She pointed to the open door. "You're supposed to get in on the passenger side and slide over to the driver's seat. Then I slide in after you. That way I can make sure you don't try anything."

"Ah," Colton said. He stepped back and closed the driver's door. "I see you've been watching plenty of crime-time television." He walked around to the passenger side of the truck, aware of her following close behind him. Opening that door, he slid in. The interior was stifling hot, so he started the engine and flipped the air-conditioning to high as the woman climbed onto the bench seat beside him. He suppressed a smile as she pulled the toy gun from her waistband and tried awkwardly to keep it trained on him while negotiating the high seat.

"Okay," she said, closing the door and turning to look at him. "Let's get out of here."

She wrestled her backpack off and let it fall to the floor. Without taking her eyes from him, she pressed herself against the door, keeping as far away from him as she could in the confines of the cab. She kept the gun low but leveled at him nonetheless.

Colton quirked an eyebrow. "Care to tell me where

we're going? You might want to make it quick, since I expect we'll have company before too long."

MADDIE HOWE TORE her gaze from the big man sitting next to her and looked beyond the parking lot to where Interstate 80 stretched away into the distance, until it was finally swallowed up by the mountains beyond. Heat shimmered in waves over that narrow ribbon of tarmac, and the plains on either side were scorched brown from the unrelenting heat of the July sun.

"Just head west toward Reno until I tell you different," she replied, shifting her gaze back to him. To her dismay, the man made no move to put the truck into gear, although one hand rested on the stick shift. He was watching her, and she thought his dark eyes held compassion.

"You sure you want to do this?" His voice was low, compelling.

Maddie swallowed nervously What if he simply refused to drive? He couldn't do that to her, she thought in near desperation. She had already come this far; had irrevocably altered her life, maybe even ruined it. For her, there was no turning back. She was committed to the course she had chosen, even if it meant ditching him and finding another driver. For her, there were no other options.

"I'm sure," she finally said, her mouth dry. Her hands tightened around the gun and she lifted it fractionally higher. "Please, just drive."

His expression told her clearly he was disappointed, but he shifted the big truck into gear and then they were pulling out onto the interstate and heading west toward the foothills of the Sierra Nevadas. Maddie spared one swift glance back at the diner, expecting what, she didn't know. It wasn't as if anyone in the place was even aware that she'd just committed a crime. The whole thing had been too easy. There was no discernible activity in the parking lot, and the rest area grew smaller and smaller as they sped away. Finally, she allowed herself to relax back into the seat.

The man beside her was silent. Maddie didn't know whether to be thankful for that or not. She watched him covertly from beneath her baseball cap. He was a big man, tall and lean with broad shoulders. He'd startled her half to death when he'd confronted her in the diner. Her first impression had been of height and width and dark eyes that had focused on her with an intensity that missed nothing.

Then he had spoken, and his voice was like a lifeline in a world that was suddenly tilting out of control. This was the kind of guy who could talk a suicide jumper down off a ledge, she decided. His voice had a quality to it that both calmed and inspired trust. It was low, and sort of rough around the edges, with a bare hint of a drawl that made you want him to keep on talking. Because when he did, you felt like he really cared. Only that was crazy, Maddie thought, because he didn't even know her. Never mind that she had kidnapped him at gunpoint.

She watched him now as he drove, his hands relaxed on the wheel. Maddie noticed he didn't wear a wedding band. She hadn't had a chance to really look at him in the diner, but now she let her eyes travel over him, lingering on his profile.

He was dark, his skin burnished to a warm copper. His black hair was cropped short in a style that was almost military. He had slashing black brows and a hawklike nose above lips that were wide and generous. Despite his chiseled cheekbones and clean, square jaw, there was an aura of toughness about him that she recognized. She was willing to bet the ladies lined up for a chance to be with him. She guessed he was at least partially Native American. Altogether, he was overwhelmingly male. He wore a black T-shirt paired with blue jeans, and it seemed his entire body was layered with muscles. Even his thighs beneath the worn denim appeared muscular.

As if sensing her scrutiny, he slanted a sideways glance at her, one black eyebrow arched in question. Maddie felt her face grow warm. What would she do if he tried to overpower her? There would be no contest. She'd be dough in his hands. She groaned inwardly. What had she been thinking to involve this man in her madness? Truth be told, she hadn't been thinking. She hadn't actually had a single coherent thought since she had received the threatening note early the previous morning, followed by the phone call. A call that had chilled her and then galvanized her into panic mode.

Her younger brother, Jamie, was in trouble. Serious trouble. He'd lost a staggering amount of money at the poker tables in Reno. Money that hadn't been his to lose. Money that the lenders now wanted back. More money than she had, despite the fact she'd emptied both her savings and checking accounts, sold her car for far less than its worth and cashed in the precious few bonds she owned.

There hadn't been nearly enough time to remortgage her little condo or apply for a bank loan. The men who were holding her brother said they would hurt him if they didn't have the money within the next seventy-two hours. And they warned her that if she involved the police, they would just kill him outright and be done with it.

Maddie believed them.

Why wouldn't she? After all, she'd seen what had happened to her father. She knew firsthand about the seamy, dark side of gambling, and what really went on in the back rooms of the casinos. But her brother was only twenty years old, just finishing up his last year of college. He'd been too young to remember what had happened to their dad, though Maddie did all too vividly.

She wouldn't let that happen to Jamie, although there was a part of her that wanted to kill him herself for having gotten into this mess. How many times had she preached to him about the dangers of gambling? She'd made him promise that he would never, under any circumstances, go to the casinos, and certainly not with money that wasn't his. But she understood the lure of turning a quick buck; of beating the house and winning huge sums of cash. Now Jamie's luck had run out, and unless she acted quickly, his life was in danger.

Frantic, she had stashed what cash she had into her backpack and boarded the first bus for Reno. She'd left a voice mail at the town office where she worked as a senior accountant, telling her boss that she had a family emergency and needed to take several days off. She had a telephone number to call once she reached Reno.

She had spent the first hundred fifty miles of the westbound bus ride tolerating the shoot-'em-up antics of the little boy in the seat in front of her. But after nearly three hours of watching him pretend to shoot her with his toy gun, her nerves had been stretched taut.

When they pulled into the rest area in Lovelock, she had spied the toy weapon lying on the seat and had quickly snatched it up, shoving it under her T-shirt and into the waistband of her jeans. She'd promised herself she would "find" the toy for the child once they reached Reno. And in the meantime have some peace and quiet.

But as she had watched the cashier at the diner laughingly ring out a customer, and glimpsed the money in the drawer, something had caught at her. Something dark and desperate, and she'd become agonizingly aware of the toy gun pressing into her stomach. Whether or not she would actually have worked up the nerve to rob the diner was something, thankfully, she would never know. What she had done was bad enough. She could scarcely believe she'd had the nerve to take this man hostage; could scarcely believe he'd been duped by the fake gun.

"Do you have a name?" the stranger was asking her, a small smile tilting the corners of his generous mouth. "Or should I just call you Bonnie?"

Maddie blinked at him. How could he be so relaxed? As far as he knew, she was pointing a loaded gun at him.

And he wanted to make jokes? In the short time they'd been driving, she had tried to decide where he should drop her. The trip to Reno would take a couple hours. Being silent and surly wasn't going to make the journey any more enjoyable, and what did it matter anyway if he knew her name? Once she had her brother safely back, she intended to turn herself in to the police. At which point everyone would know who she was.

"Madeleine," she answered shortly, not adding that people generally called her Maddie.

"I'm Colton Black," he drawled. "I'm real sorry we couldn't have met under different circumstances."

To Maddie's horror, he extended a hand to her across the seat. It was large and tanned, with lean fingers tapering to neat nails. She raised her gaze to his, keeping her expression blank. He was watching her carefully, while keeping an eye on the almost empty road.

Did he really believe she was that big of a fool? She knew what would happen if she shook that hand. He'd haul her across the seat and wrest her miserable excuse for a weapon from her nerveless fingers. No, thank you.

But he only grinned and pulled his hand back. "Okay," he murmured, as if talking to himself. "That's okay. You're not ready to be sociable yet. I understand. But here we are, just you and me." He gave a wry smile. "At least we're heading in the right direction."

Maddie blinked. "Excuse me?"

He slanted a swift look at her. "I was headed up to Paradise Valley for a couple of weeks of fishing. I'll drop you wherever it is you want to go, and maybe I can still reach my cabin before it gets too late."

Maddie stared at him in disbelief. "I can't let you go. You know that."

He kept his gaze straight ahead. "Why not? I promise you, darlin', you sure as hell don't want the kind of trouble I'll bring you."

Was that a threat or just a general comment about the hazards of taking hostages? Maddie pressed herself closer against the passenger door. "Look, I really don't want any trouble. I—I just need to do something, okay? Once it's done, I'll let you go."

"Oh, yeah?" A small smile lifted one corner of his mouth. "What's so important that you'd risk your life, huh? Why were you going to hold up the diner? Is it drugs?" His gaze swept over her, sharply assessing. "Or do you need to pay off a bookie?"

Maddie blanched at his words, but he'd turned his attention back to the road and didn't see her sudden panic. She glanced out the window at the desert rushing past. As soon as he'd mentioned his cabin in Paradise Valley, she'd known exactly what she needed to do. Her grandfather had a cabin in the hills, and he'd once said that he had a fortune hidden there. She had no idea if that was true, but she needed to check it out, although it required turning off the main road. But she couldn't afford to have her focus diverted by this man. She needed to unload him and get on with her mission. If she ditched him here, on the main road, he'd have a better chance of hitching a ride with someone. Her conscience wouldn't allow her to leave him in the foothills, where a day's hike without sufficient water could mean death in these temperatures.

"Pull the truck over." Her voice sounded low and strained, even to her own ears.

Colton gave a disbelieving laugh. "What?"

Maddie jabbed the gun in his direction. "You heard me. I said pull over."

His lips compressed as he steered the truck off the road and onto the soft shoulder in a cloud of billowing dust. He thrust the vehicle into Park, but didn't turn off the engine.

"Now what?" He turned his head slowly and gave her a level look. "You tell me to get out and I start hiking across the desert?" He shook his head. "Ain't going to happen, lady. Besides, I thought you said you couldn't let me go."

Maddie frowned. "I've—I've changed my mind. I don't need you, just your truck." She made a motion with the gun, willing her hands not to tremble. "Get out. You don't have to walk across the desert or anything, you just have to get out. Someone will come by eventually, and you can hitch a ride."

She watched, stunned, as he laughed softly. He turned to her, still grinning. She tried to ignore the mesmerizing dimples that appeared in either lean cheek.

"No way, ma'am. Absolutely no freaking way am I getting out of this truck."

Maddie stared at him. "What are you, crazy?" She gestured threateningly with the toy gun. "I could shoot you right now."

He spread his arms wide. "Well, then, you go right ahead, darlin', because the only way I'm leaving this truck is if I'm dead."

Maddie blinked, appalled. "You're not serious."

"I sure as hell am." He slapped the dashboard. "This baby is brand-new. I worked damned hard for her, and there's no way I'm giving her up. You want her, you gotta shoot me first."

This couldn't really be happening. Maddie swept a trembling hand across her eyes, trying to hide the panic she was feeling. She couldn't afford to have this man involved, didn't want him involved. She glanced again at the seemingly endless expanse of desert that stretched away to the foothills of the Sierra Nevadas. Even if *she* chose to leave the truck, she'd never make it across those heat-baked plains on foot.

She turned her attention back to the man beside her. He was staring out the window, drumming his fingers against his thigh in tune to some internal melody, as if he hadn't a care in the world. As if she wasn't capable of shooting him.

Which she wasn't, because her gun was nothing more than a child's toy. He might not know that, but somehow he intuitively knew she didn't have what it took to commit cold-blooded murder.

She blew out her breath in frustration and sagged back against the seat, making no protest when he shifted gears and pulled the truck back onto the highway.

"Fine," she conceded, trying to sound as if she still maintained control. "You leave me no choice but to take you with me."

He flashed her a swift grin. "No kidding. So where to?"

"Take the next turnoff, and follow the signs to Spotted Canyon."

"Okay then," he murmured, almost to himself. "This could still work out okay. We're still headed in the general direction of Paradise Valley. I'll just drop you off wherever it is you're going, and then I'll head to my cabin."

Maddie almost choked on the spurt of semihysterical laughter that burst forth before she quickly composed herself. She couldn't believe he was still preoccupied with reaching his cabin. She didn't respond, but instead stared resolutely through the windshield, determined to ignore him.

"So," he continued conversationally, "what's a nice girl like you doing in a situation like this?"

Maddie slanted him one look of warning before turning her attention back to the road. She pointed to a turn-off that was barely discernible in the distance.

"Take this next right."

Colton looked at her in surprise. "You sure it's this one?"

It was a dirt road, surrounded on either side by brush and rocky terrain. Maddie knew that it wound steadily upward into the foothills. It had been several years since she'd traveled it, but there was no doubt in her mind this was the correct road.

"Yes, I'm sure. Now do you mind if we don't talk, and just drive?"

"Sure."

She breathed a sigh of relief when they turned onto the dirt road, one of hundreds of narrow, rutted routes that twisted their way through the hills.

When she had first boarded the Greyhound bus back

in Elko, she had planned on traveling straight through to Reno. She would figure out how to get her brother back once she got there. But then, of course, she'd made the stupid, stupid mistake of taking this man hostage. She'd been formulating a plan on how to come up with the cash she needed, and it involved gambling, but she couldn't very well waltz into one of the casinos with this man strapped to her side. She'd been in near despair as to what her next course of action should be, when he'd mentioned a cabin in Paradise Valley.

It was then that she knew what she had to do.

2

COLTON GLANCED OVER at the woman. She was slumped against the door, and he could see she was having trouble keeping her eyes open. She held the gun loosely in her lap. They'd been driving for nearly four hours, negotiating the uneven dirt roads that threaded their way through the foothills of the Sierra Nevadas and climbed steadily upward into the more heavily timbered forests. Several times she had directed him to take a certain turn, but had otherwise been silent.

"It's going to be dark soon," he commented. "I don't know about you, but I hear nature calling. Mind if we stop for a quick break?"

She didn't look at him. "Can't you hold it?"

"Nope."

Turning her head, she gave him an assessing look. "Okay, but it has to be quick. We're almost there."

"Almost where?" He gave a rueful laugh. "Looks like we're out in the middle of nowhere."

"I know exactly where we are," she answered tersely. "You can pull over here."

He stopped the truck and was about to get out when she surprised him by laying a hand on his arm. He paused and looked first at the slender fingers, and then at her, arching an eyebrow in query.

She actually blushed, and then snatched her hand back as if it had been burned. "I'll take the keys."

Colton glanced down at the set in his hand, then shrugged and dropped them into her lap. "Fine. But if you're thinking you're going to leave me here, I'd reconsider. We're almost out of gas."

He heard her sharp intake of breath. "Why didn't you say so?"

"What would be the point? It's not like there's a gas station beyond the next bend."

"How much farther do you think we can drive with the gas we have left?" Her voice was low, but Colton could hear traces of anxiety.

"Fifteen miles. Maybe. We're on rock bottom empty." He didn't tell her he had a reserve tank that would get them an additional fifty miles. He watched with interest as her entire body seemed to sag with relief at his words.

"That's more than enough. We only have another five or so to go, and I know there's an old gas station on the other side of this mountain. At least," she amended, turning to gaze distractedly out the window, "there used to be."

Colton wondered how long it had been since she'd traveled through this area, and why she needed to reach Reno. He climbed out of the cab and was just about to step away from the road and into the nearby woods when her voice stopped him.

"Right there is fine."

He angled a glance at her over his shoulder. She leaned across the bench seat and was once more aiming the useless gun at him. "What, now you want to watch?" He injected just enough derision into his voice to make the color bloom in her cheeks.

"Of course not. I just want to keep you in sight. I won't look."

Colton sighed. "How about I just step in front of the truck with my back to you?" She nodded, and he moved to stand in front of the hood. He discreetly relieved himself, acutely aware of the amber eyes that watched him from behind the windshield.

As he prepared to climb back behind the wheel, she lowered the pistol and began fiddling with the latch on his glove compartment. "I don't suppose you have anything to eat stashed in here, do you? A candy bar or something?"

Alarm bells jangled in Colton's head as he recalled exactly what he had stashed in the glove box: his service revolver and a two-way radio. He couldn't let her find either, or the game, such as it was, would definitely be up. He didn't doubt his own ability to overpower her if she should get her hands on the weapon, but neither did he trust her to handle it responsibly. She could shoot him without meaning to.

"Nothing but junk in there," he assured her quickly, "but I do have some water and snacks in the back. If you'll let me, I'll be happy to grab some for us."

Her hands fell away from the glove compartment, and she gave him a brief ghost of a smile. "Thanks."

He retrieved two bottles of water and a bag of pretzels from beneath the canvas tarp. He tossed them lightly onto her lap and held out his hands for the keys. She snatched up one of the bottles, uncapped it and drank greedily for a long moment before she finally noticed his waiting hand. Slowly, she lowered the bottle.

"Sorry," she mumbled. "I guess I was thirstier than I realized."

She handed him the keys, and Colton pulled back onto the road, but he was conscious of the woman as she drained the water bottle and started in on the pretzels.

"When did you last eat?" he asked, keeping his voice casual.

Madeleine, nibbling on a pretzel, flushed. "I don't remember. Yesterday, I think."

"You think?"

"It's been a crazy couple of days. Eating didn't seem to be a priority." Her tone was defensive. "Oh! Turn here."

She indicated a road that was little more than an overgrown trail. If she hadn't pointed it out to him, Colton might not have seen it. Branches and underbrush dragged along the side of the truck as he made his way along the road, and he winced inwardly, wondering what it was doing to the finish. He wasn't fussy by nature, but he hadn't lied when he'd told her the truck was brand-new. He'd barely broken it in.

Suddenly, the trail opened up, and a clearing lay ahead. Colton leaned forward to peer through the windshield. There was an enormous boulder flanked by aspen and cottonwood trees, and near it a small cabin.

Colton thought he'd never seen a place so perfectly situated in the natural beauty surrounding it.

It was a simple log structure with a porch on the front. It faced west across the small clearing to where the pine trees suddenly vanished at the edge of a steep precipice. Spread out before them was a breathtaking panoramic view of the Santa Rosa Mountains in the distance. The sun had dipped just below the horizon, and the blaze of colors that streaked the sky over the peaks stole his breath. Colton drew the truck alongside the small cabin and simply stared.

"I'll take the keys," Madeleine said to him, and he handed them to her almost absently.

"Christ," he murmured, "this place is unbelievable."

But she had already climbed out of the cab. Colton watched as she shoved the keys into the front pocket of her jeans, and the toy gun into her waistband. She took the steps to the porch two at a time.

He let his gaze travel over the cabin. It was obviously abandoned. Signs of disuse and neglect were apparent in the thick coating of leaves and pine needles that covered the porch and roof, as well as the green moss that had begun to take root on the log walls.

Slowly, he got out of the truck and followed Madeleine. She was on her knees in front of the door, brushing aside leaves and other debris as she searched beneath an ancient mat. When she didn't find what she was looking for—the keys, Colton suspected—she stood up and began forcibly trying to open the door. When jiggling and pushing the handle didn't work, she applied her shoulder, grunting each time she threw her weight against the solid planking. Still, the door didn't budge.

She was going to hurt herself if she kept it up. Colton didn't know who the cabin belonged to, or why it was so important to her that she gain access, but he suspected it was more than just a place to hide out.

"Here," he said, and nudged her to one side. He studied the door for a moment and then, standing back, drew his leg up and kicked with the heel of his booted foot, just to the side of the handle. The door exploded inward, shearing the interior dead bolt from the frame.

Colton looked at Madeleine, who was staring at the scene with an expression of awe. She turned to him.

"That was quite…impressive. Thanks."

"No problem," he murmured. "Just call me Clyde. If I'm not mistaken, this makes me an accomplice."

"Nonsense. I'll tell anyone who asks that I forced you to do it."

Without waiting for his response, she stepped into the cabin. Colton followed, brushing aside cobwebs that had accumulated across the doorway.

"So, on top of aggravated kidnapping, we now add breaking and entering to your growing list of crimes," he said sardonically, watching as she took a dusty kerosene lantern down from a hook inside the door.

She set it on a nearby table, ignoring him as she carefully adjusted the wick and then lit it with a long match that she drew from a tin box next to the lantern. The bright flame slowly grew into a soft, warm glow, chasing away the shadows that surrounded them and casting golden light across her features.

"You can't be accused of breaking and entering when you own the house," she finally said, looking up at him.

Colton couldn't hide his surprise. "This is your place?"

"Yeah. At least since my grandpa died. Here, hold this." She handed him the lantern, and he followed her into the adjoining kitchen. It was small and dark with knotty pine cupboards and an ancient cookstove in one corner. Colton watched as she yanked open a drawer and began rummaging through an assortment of silverware. He arched a brow when she drew forth a stout knife.

To his surprise, she dropped to her knees beside the stove, brushed aside the accumulated dust and began tracing the wide pine floorboards with her fingers. Then she slid the knife between two of the boards and attempted to pry one up. When it refused to budge, she cursed and flung the knife into a corner.

She scrambled to her feet, and as she dug through the silverware drawer once more, Colton slipped out of the room. Keeping an eye on the entrance to the cabin, he retrieved a crowbar from the back of the trunk. He would have liked to retrieve his police radio and contact his boss. But he didn't want to risk her seeing him, or suspect he was anything more than a cooperative hostage.

Yet.

When he reentered the kitchen, she was on her knees again, this time working at the floorboards with some kind of barbecue skewer. It was no more effective than the knife had been.

"Here, let me try." He crouched beside her.

She had taken her baseball cap off in the truck. Her hair had come partially free of her ponytail and hung in disarray around her flushed face. Her expression of dismay as she took in the crowbar was almost comical. Horror and then relief flitted across her face, and Colton knew she was thinking he could easily have overpowered her.

Before she could protest, he inserted the end of the crowbar between the planks and wrenched upward. Setting the bar aside, he used his hands to wrest the boards up, pulling them free and tossing them aside. He had a glimpse of a shallow storage area beneath the floor.

With a glad cry, Madeleine reached into the space and withdrew what looked to be an ancient holiday cookie tin. It was covered in dust and mottled with rust. As Colton watched, she pried the top off and spilled the contents onto the kitchen floor. There was a thick wad of folded money among the various items, and with a soft gasp she snatched it up and carried it over to the kitchen table to count it.

Crouching on the balls of his feet, Colton traced a finger through the remaining items. There were several photos, some yellowed and cracked with age, and others that were more recent. He picked one up and tilted it toward the lantern. It was a picture of a girl, maybe thirteen or fourteen years old, sitting on the front steps of the cabin. She had her arm slung around the shoulders of a little boy. They were both skinny, with sun-browned skin and fair hair. He glanced over at Madeleine. It was her, taken maybe fifteen years earlier. Based on the similarity between them, he guessed the little boy was her brother.

There was a photo of an older Madeleine and a frail old man with a grizzled beard. Colton estimated it had been taken no more than a couple years ago. In it she wore a simple sundress, and he raised an eyebrow at the length of leg exposed by the style. He surreptitiously pocketed the photos.

He sorted through the remaining items—a slender length of chain with a small key attached to it, several coins, a handful of poker chips, some old lottery tickets, and what looked to be the deed to the cabin and surrounding land. Colton picked up the key and turned it over in his hand before slipping it into his pocket with the pilfered photos.

He glanced up as Madeleine started laughing. The money was spread out on the table in front of her and Colton could see it was mostly small denomination bills. Her laughter grew, became slightly hysterical. Just when he thought he was going to have to intervene, she buried her face in her hands and the laughter turned to deep, racking sobs.

Colton guessed there wasn't as much money hidden away beneath the floorboards as she had hoped, and wondered again what the nature of her problem was. He had initially suspected drugs, though he admitted to himself she didn't seem the type. In fact, she radiated good health. Even with the oversize shirt and no cosmetics, she was more than just attractive. Her hair was a silken mass of dark gold with wheaten streaks, and for one brief instant he wondered what it would feel like under his hands. He had seen the evidence of her slender curves in the photo. There wasn't anything about her that wasn't completely feminine. Colton thought she might be breathtaking if she would only smile.

Pushing himself to his feet, he stood uncertainly for a moment. The racking sobs subsided, but she still cried quietly into her hands. The hysterical laughter and deep sobs he could handle. Her soft weeping nearly undid him.

He took one step toward her, then spun away, raking a hand over his hair. He swung back, staring at her bent head and trembling shoulders. The urge to take her in his arms and comfort her was almost overwhelming. He was actually standing over her, one hand poised above her hair, before he realized what he was doing and managed to get a grip on himself. While she might rouse every protective instinct he had, nothing good could come of letting himself feel anything for her. With a muttered curse, he turned on his heel and strode from the cabin.

SHE WAS A fool to have believed the cabin would hold the key to her brother's release. When her grandfather had become too frail to continue living alone in the cabin, Maddie had made the difficult decision to move him to a nursing home in Elko, where she could visit him every day. Toward the end, he'd suffered from acute dementia, insisting he needed to return to his cabin. He claimed he had a fortune hidden there.

Maddie knew about the tin box he kept hidden beneath the floorboards. Her grandfather had stashed his spare money there for years, but it had never, to her knowledge, amounted to much. Even though the rational part of her brain insisted the tin contained little, if anything, of value, her grandfather's words had come back to her. During the ride into the mountains, she had actually begun to fantasize that perhaps he had somehow managed to put away a substantial hoard of cash.

She was such an idiot.

Maddie drew in a shuddering breath and swiped her palms across her wet cheeks. The money lay in a messy heap on the table. Her heart had leaped when she first saw the thick wad of bills inside the tin, but hope had turned to despair when she realized there was barely five hundred dollars there. Even combined with what she had, it didn't come close to satisfying the debt her brother owed. She glanced over at the gaping hole in the floor and the scattered contents of the tin. But it wasn't until her gaze fell on the discarded crowbar that she remembered.

Colton.

While she had been crying her heart out over the lack of money in the tin, he had slipped away. With her luck, he had a spare key and had taken the truck, as well. She couldn't afford to be stranded here. With her heart slamming in her chest, Maddie leaped to her feet and bolted from the room. In the deepening shadows of early evening, she nearly collided with Colton as he reentered the cabin, carrying a large cardboard box.

"Oh! I thought you were gone, that you'd taken the truck." She felt a little weak with relief.

In the indistinct light, he peered at her. "I'm not going to get too far without my keys, am I?" He indicated the box in his arms. "It's getting dark, and with the gas tank on empty, we're not going anywhere tonight. I have two weeks' worth of food and supplies in the bed of the truck. I thought the least I could do was fix us something to eat."

Still flustered by her own incompetence, Maddie followed him back into the kitchen and watched as he set the box of provisions on the table, sweeping the money aside with a careless gesture.

"How about some sandwiches? I have ham or roast beef." He glanced at her over his shoulder as he spoke, pulling bread and condiments out of the box.

Maddie hesitated. There was no way she was going to spend the night here at the cabin. She couldn't afford to waste any more time. Her overactive imagination conjured up lurid images of what the moneylenders might do to her brother. He was still such a kid. Jamie might act cocky, but Maddie knew that's all it was—an act. He must be scared to death. She desperately needed to come up with fifty thousand dollars in cash, and she couldn't do that here in this cabin. Jamie was the only family she had left in the world. She'd practically raised him since he was a toddler, and she wouldn't abandon him now when he desperately needed her.

But the sight of the food that Colton was pulling out of the box reminded her how long it had been since she'd last eaten anything substantial. Surely an hour or so couldn't do any harm, and she needed to eat something. She had to keep her strength up if she was going to help Jamie.

"Fine," she replied. "But we're not spending the night. As soon as we finish eating, we'll head down the other side of the mountain. I'm sure that old gas station is still there."

She saw a muscle flex in Colton's jaw, but he didn't say anything. As he fixed the sandwiches in silence, Maddie got the pump working and made short work of wiping down the kitchen surfaces. They sat at the small table and ate by the glow of the kerosene lantern. She thought she'd never tasted anything as delicious as the thick ham sandwiches he'd prepared for them. She finished eating and sank gratefully back in her chair, satisfied. The toy gun dug painfully into her stomach where it was still tucked into her waistband. She was tempted to place it on the table, but was reluctant to destroy the uneasy camaraderie she and her hostage shared. Besides, she couldn't risk Colton taking it from her.

He sat back in his chair and drained the remnants of a water bottle he'd retrieved from an enormous cooler. Maddie couldn't help it; she stared, fascinated by the muscles working in the strong column of his throat. He set the empty bottle on the table, laced his hands across his flat belly and arched an eyebrow at her.

Maddie flushed and looked away, more uncertain than she'd been since this whole nightmare started. She cleared her throat. "We should go before it gets too dark. There's a tank of gasoline in the shed. Maybe enough to get us down the mountain."

She risked a glance at him. He was watching her

carefully, his expression a mixture of compassion and resignation. He leaned forward and placed his palms on the table.

"Look," he began, "we've both had a long day. It's late and it's dark, and we don't know if this gas station you're talking about even exists anymore." He studied his hands for a moment, before turning his dark gaze back to her. "I don't know what kind of trouble you're in, but it's obvious you need some help." He held up a palm to forestall her when she would have spoken. "I think the best thing you can do now is get a good night's sleep. In the morning, I'll drive you into Winnemucca and you can turn yourself in to the local authorities."

Maddie was helpless to prevent the soft gasp of dismay that escaped her. "What?"

He held his hands up in a supplicating gesture. "Listen to me, Madeleine. You have no food, no car, and I'm guessing not much money. What you've done by taking me with you is considered a felony. You could find yourself behind bars for a long time. Whatever the problem is, you're only going to make it worse by running."

He was doing it again; speaking in a way that was almost hypnotic. His tone was soothing and rational without being patronizing. Maddie had an overwhelming urge to fling herself against his broad chest and tell him she'd do anything he wanted.

She lifted her chin and met his gaze squarely. "I can't go to the police." She hated the way her voice quavered, despite her resolve to remain in control. "You don't understand." She gave a laugh of disbelief. "There's absolutely no way I can involve the authorities."

Colton sighed. "I'm sorry, Madeleine, but you already have."

Before she knew what he was doing, he reached into the back pocket of his jeans and drew forth a slim wallet. He flipped it open and held it out for her to see.

Appalled, Maddie stared at the badge inside. It was a silver star inside a silver circle, with the words United States Deputy Marshal emblazoned in blue around it. On the opposite side of the wallet was an identification card with Colton's picture beneath a federal seal of office.

She felt the blood drain from her face as she raised her eyes to look at him. "You're a U.S. Marshal?" Her voice was scarcely more than a husky whisper.

"The game's up, Madeleine."

3

MADDIE LUNGED TO her feet so fast that she knocked her chair over. She fumbled frantically for the toy gun in her waistband. Yanking it free, she pointed it at Colton, even as she backed away from him.

"Don't touch me!" Her voice sounded shrill. Desperate. She felt ill. To her dismay, he stood up and took a step toward her, looking completely unfazed by the gun. "I mean it." she said, jabbing the weapon at him. "I'll—I'll shoot you if you take another step."

His smile seemed almost regretful. "C'mon, Madeleine, don't do this."

Maddie stepped backward and came up against the edge of the counter. She felt ridiculously close to tears again. This couldn't be happening. She couldn't allow herself to be arrested. "Stop right there. I'll shoot, I swear it."

But Colton didn't stop until he was just inches away from her, with the barrel of the gun pressing hard into his midsection.

"So shoot," he said softly.

Maddie stared up at him. His eyes were so dark they were almost black, but the empathy she saw there nearly undid her. A sob born of panic and frustration was torn from her, and then his hand was covering her own, pulling the useless weapon out of her fingers. "I know it's a fake, Madeleine. You were never going to shoot me because it's not a real gun."

Maddie gasped. "You knew? Since when?"

"Since the diner."

She stared at him in disbelief. "You knew all this time? And yet you came with me anyway? All this time, and you just let me go on thinking—" Her free hand flew to her mouth. "Oh, God, I'm such an idiot."

His hand still covered hers, and now his other arm slid behind her shoulders. He pulled her against his chest, murmuring words of comfort into her hair.

She hadn't even been aware she was crying until he massaged the back of her neck and his husky voice curled around her. "Don't cry. Please don't cry. It'll be okay. Shh. Don't cry."

Her face was pressed against the muscled hardness of his chest, and his arms encircled her. She thought she could willingly stay like this forever. God, he smelled good, like clean laundry and the outdoors, mixed with a tangy scent that was his alone. But it was the way he made her feel that was having the strangest effect on her senses. She could hear the steady thud of his heart beneath her ear. He was strong and solid, and it felt so good to lean against him. For the first time in her life, she felt protected. As if she could finally relinquish all the burdens she'd been carrying for so many years and just breathe.

"It'll be okay," he said. "Whatever the problem is, we'll figure it out. I'll make sure the police know I came with you of my own free will. I'm sure they'll go easy on you."

Maddie froze.

In an instant, all the good feelings vanished, leaving her cold inside. She pulled free of his arms and pushed past him to stand on the opposite side of the small kitchen. She swiped furiously at her cheeks.

"So what now?" she asked scathingly. "I'm just supposed to go with you to the authorities and let them put me in prison?"

Colton frowned, and even in her distress, Maddie recognized the real concern in his dark eyes. "They won't put you in prison, Madeleine. I promise you that. The worst case scenario is you post bail until your court appearance, and you'll get a suspended sentence with community service."

She gave a short laugh that sounded slightly hysterical again. "You've got to be kidding." She pressed her fingers against her eyes. "This is unbelievable. It can't really be happening."

"Madeleine." He was standing directly in front of her now. "Talk to me. Tell me what's going on. Maybe I can help you."

His image wavered through the tears that filled her eyes. She smiled tremulously. "You can't help me. Nobody can."

"Well, I sure as hell can't help you if you don't tell

me what the problem is. Explain to me why you were planning to hold up a diner."

"I don't know!" she cried. "There was that little boy on the bus, and he was playing with his toy gun, pretending to shoot me with it. I was sick of it, and when he left the gun on the seat, I just took it. I would have given it back to him in Reno."

"But instead, you decided that robbing the diner was a good idea."

"Yes. No!" She groaned and closed her eyes for a moment. "I don't know what I was thinking. I saw the money in the register, and I had this gun in my belt, and—I'm not even sure if I could have gone through with it."

"So you wanted the money," he said flatly. "Why?"

Maddie turned away from him. She couldn't think straight when he was so close, so authoritative and demanding. There must be some way to get away from him and avoid being turned over to the authorities in the morning. Even if the police were willing to help her, she couldn't risk having them involved. The men who had her brother had said they would kill him if she called the police, and she believed them.

She just needed to get Jamie back safely, and then she'd willingly go to the police. But first she had to ditch the U.S. marshal, no matter how well meaning he might be.

"Okay," she finally said, and drew in a deep breath as she spun around to face him. "You're right. I want to end this thing, too." She forced herself to smile, injecting what she hoped was just the right amount of regret and resignation into her expression. She held her wrists out to him. "Do you want to handcuff me to the bed tonight…you know, to make sure I don't run away?"

Colton's eyes widened fractionally, and Maddie was certain she saw his mouth twitch in amusement. "Uh, no," he finally said. "I don't think that will be necessary." He gave her a lopsided grin. "I'm a light sleeper. You wouldn't make it to the door. But just in case—" he held out his hand "—I'll have my keys back."

With a sigh, she fished his keys out of her pocket and handed them to him, then watched as he pocketed them in turn.

She wrapped her arms around her middle, hugging herself. Her eyes ached and her stomach felt hollow. "So now what?"

"Now you get to answer my questions. Why do you need money?"

Maddie glanced at him. His expression was inscrutable, but his jaw was set in hard lines. She didn't dare tell him the truth, because if he decided to get involved, it could mean even worse trouble for Jamie. If she had learned one thing from her unconventional upbringing, it was to always stick as close to the truth as possible. If you told too many lies, you'd become so embroiled in them that you would lose track of what was real and what was fiction.

"I have some outstanding debt," she finally said. "If I don't pay the money I owe, I could lose everything."

"Who do you owe the money to?"

"The bank," she replied, tipping her chin up. "I got behind on some payments."

"That's it?"

She shrugged. "That's it."

His eyes narrowed as he considered her, and then he turned abruptly away. "It gets pretty chilly in the mountains, even at this time of year. Why don't I get a fire started for us while you check out the sleeping arrangements?"

Maddie watched him. Did he believe her? She didn't know. What she did know was that she wouldn't be spending the night at the cabin. She had no time to waste, and she certainly wasn't about to go willingly with him to Winnemucca. But she had to at least give the appearance of acquiescence.

"Okay, fine. There's a loft over the living room where I used to sleep when I was a kid. My grandpa's old bedroom is just beneath that."

"Great. I'll go check out the loft."

Maddie followed him into the living room and watched as he lit several more lanterns. As the soft light slowly chased away the last of the shadows, she had to swallow hard against the sudden constriction in her throat. The place hadn't changed at all in the years since she'd lived here as a kid. There was the old mission oak sofa with the plaid fabric and sturdy wooden arms, the braided rug, her grandpa's favorite reading chair next to the stone fireplace. The flowered curtains she'd made as a teenager still hung in the windows.

Despite the homey feel of the room, Madeleine couldn't summon any warm memories of the place. She'd been ten years old when her mother had died of cancer, and she hadn't thought life could get any worse.

But she'd been wrong. Now, looking around the small cabin, all she could remember was the horror she'd felt after her father's sudden death, when she'd understood that this was to be her new home, living with a grandfather she barely knew. At first, she'd been terrified of his gruff manner, but she'd soon learned that he was just a pathetic old man incapable of taking care of himself, never mind a twelve-year-old girl and a three-year-old boy. Her grandpa would drink until he passed out, leaving Maddie to fend for herself.

Unwilling to leave Jamie alone in the cabin with their unconscious grandfather, she'd take him with her down the mountain and hang around outside Zeke's place. Back then, old Zeke had run the only gas station and general store in the area, and Maddie had discovered that she could often wheedle a few bucks out of sympathetic locals and vacationing tourists. Enough to buy a few groceries for herself and her brother.

As she'd gotten older, her grandfather had made several attempts to get sober, and those were the days Maddie preferred to remember. When there was enough food in the cupboards that she didn't need to con money out of strangers, and she and Jamie would spend the long evenings playing blackjack or poker under their grandpa's skillful tutelage. But his periods of sobriety were few and short-lived, and she'd learned not to expect too much from him.

She preferred it that way. She didn't want to depend on anyone. Not even a gorgeous, well-meaning U.S. marshal.

Colton was currently examining the narrow ladder

that stood in one corner of the room and served as the only access to a small sleeping loft overhead. He tested it with his weight before negotiating the rungs, holding a lantern aloft as he did so.

Maddie stood by the sofa and watched the light bob against the roof timbers as he moved around. His face appeared over the railing. "I wouldn't recommend either of us sleep up here," he called down to her. "Looks like the mice have pretty much taken over."

"I'll check out the bedroom. Maybe you can sleep in there, and I can take the couch."

He quirked his lips and she flushed. Okay, so that was completely transparent, but it would be that much more difficult to sneak out of the cabin if *he* was on the couch. Before he could speak, she moved across the room and pushed open the door to the bedroom.

An iron bed frame draped with a dust cloth dominated the small room. Carefully, Maddie pulled the protective covering off, wadded it up and tossed it onto a chair in the corner. The pillows and bright quilt that had been hidden beneath the cloth were exactly as she remembered. The bed linens might smell a bit musty, but they were clean and serviceable.

Next to the bedroom was a tiny bathroom. Maddie grimaced at the host of spiders that had taken up residence in the shower stall. She turned on the water in the sink and let it run until it was clear, meanwhile pressing her fingers against her temples, feeling a headache begin to throb behind her eyes. She opened the medicine cabinet over the sink, hoping to find a bottle of aspirin or painkillers. There was a razor, a can of shaving cream, an outdated prescription bottle of sleeping tablets and a toothbrush, but no aspirin.

She closed the cabinet door, and catching sight of her reflection in the mirror, gasped in dismay.

She was a wreck.

Her hair had come almost completely free of its ponytail and hung haphazardly around her face, which was blotchy from crying. Her eyes were red-rimmed, and there were dark circles beneath them that made her look tired and defeated. Had it really been just one day since she'd received the phone call about her brother? She felt as if she'd aged years since then.

Just thinking about what Jamie might be suffering at the hands of the extortionists made her heart thump hard in fear. She needed to get away from Colton Black, and find a way to come up with the money needed to free her brother.

She yanked off the ponytail holder and ran her fingers through her hair, trying to restore some order to the tangled mass. She finally secured it into a loose knot on the back of her head, then bent to scoop cold water into her hands, splashing it against her face.

She could hear Colton moving around in the outer room, and peeked through the bedroom doorway just in time to see him cross to the fireplace with an enormous armful of firewood. Slowly, she lowered the face towel she was using and stared.

The man positively bulged with muscles. He set the wood down and crouched on his haunches beside the hearth to build a fire. His T-shirt rode up slightly in the back as he leaned forward, affording her a glimpse of smooth, coppery skin. She watched the play of muscles across his broad shoulders as he worked, remembering how it had felt to be pressed against all that firm, solid warmth.

Maddie turned back to the mirror and slowly finished drying her face. Before she could change her mind, she dragged the T-shirt off, pulling it over her head and tossing it through the open door onto the foot of the bed. Beneath it she wore a thin cotton tank top that clung to her curves, clearly outlining her breasts. Leaning forward, she studied her reflection critically in the mirror. She pulled several tendrils of hair loose from the knot, letting them trail along her neck. She pinched some color into her pale cheeks and bit her lips until they were rosy. Standing back, she dipped her chin and practiced her best come-hither look.

She groaned aloud and buried her face in her hands.

She'd been a desperate teenager the last time she'd used her looks for personal gain, and she wondered if she still had the ability to exploit herself. Of course, she'd been little more than a kid back then, willing to do anything to keep what was left of her family together. But she'd put all that behind her the day she left the mountains. Her troubled childhood and tainted family history were a thing of the past. These days, she was respected by the people she worked with, and her skill with numbers had earned her a good job as a lead accountant in the town of Elko. She wondered what her coworkers would think if they could see her now.

Maddie drew in a deep breath and raised her head to stare solemnly at her reflection. Jamie was depending on her, as he had his entire life. She would do anything to ensure his safety.

Slowly, she reopened the medicine cabinet. Her hand hesitated briefly, then she took down the bottle of sleeping tablets. They had been prescribed for her grandfather four years earlier, when the demons of his past had finally caught up with him. Normally, he'd have turned to the bottle and drunk himself into oblivion, but his advanced liver disease made that option a guaranteed death sentence.

Glancing guiltily toward the living room, Maddie opened the bottle. How many pills would it take to impact a man of Colton's size? And did they even have any potency left? She didn't want to kill him, just knock him out long enough to make her escape. She shook four capsules into the palm of her hand, hesitated briefly, and then shook out three more. She broke them open and emptied the powdery contents into the shallow cap of the bottle, and concealed it in the palm of her hand, careful not to spill any. Then, taking a deep breath, she walked out to the living room.

Colton was still crouched by the hearth, where a small fire was beginning to crackle. Combined with the kerosene lamps on the mantel and side tables, it gave the room a warm, almost cozy feel.

Maddie curled up at one end of the sofa and tucked her feet beneath her as she watched Colton add two more logs to the fledgling fire. He stood up and brushed his hands against his thighs.

"That should help keep us comfortable tonight," he

commented, but his voice trailed off as he finally looked at her.

Maddie felt suddenly exposed in the skimpy, sleeveless top, and she wished she'd kept her T-shirt on. More than that, she felt cheap. Did he see right through her ruse? She forced herself to meet his eyes, but his expression was shuttered.

"Yes, I'd forgotten how chilly the nights can get in the mountains, but it feels warm in here." She gestured toward the bedroom. "I'll sleep in my grandfather's room, if you don't mind taking the couch. I'll see if there's a spare pillow and blanket in the closet."

Colton sat down on the opposite end of the sofa, turning slightly toward her and laying one arm along the back. "I've slept in worse places. Don't worry about me. I have a sleeping bag out in the truck."

Maddie drew in a deep breath. If she was going to do this, she had better get on with it. There was no telling how long it would be before the sleeping pills took effect, and she didn't want to spend the entire night waiting for him to pass out.

She pushed herself to her feet. "I—I'm a little nervous about what will happen to me tomorrow. I probably won't sleep a wink, worrying about it." She moved to a small built-in cabinet beside the fireplace and opened the doors, revealing several bottles of hard liquor and some small glasses. She took two glasses down and selected a bottle of Kentucky bourbon from the shelf. Turning slightly toward Colton, she held up the bottle. "I'm going to have a small glass. It will calm my nerves and help me sleep." She hesitated. "Will you join me, or are you on duty?"

She could feel his eyes narrow in speculation, as if if was trying to figure out what she was up to. Finally, he shrugged.

"Just a splash for me, no more."

Maddie turned quickly away, lest he see the relief on her face. If he'd chosen not to have the drink, she would have had to come up with another plan. Swiftly, using her body as a shield, she surreptitiously dumped the contents of the shallow cap into his glass. She splashed a liberal amount of bourbon on top, and then gave the liquid a quick stir with her finger, hoping the garish design painted on the outside of the glass would effectively disguise any sediment that might remain. She poured two fingers for herself and carried both glasses to the couch, settling herself back on the cushions.

"Cheers," she said, and handed Colton's glass to him. She took a sip, deliberately not looking at him as he quaffed the entire shot in one swallow.

"Whoa!" he gasped, as he set the empty glass down on the table beside the couch. "I've never been much of a bourbon drinker, and now I remember why. That's awful."

Maddie looked guiltily at her own drink. He'd definitely noticed the bitter taste of the pills, and she hoped he didn't suspect it was anything more than the cheap brand of bourbon. What if he picked up the empty glass and examined the residue that must surely be visible on the bottom? What if the powder hadn't dissolved sufficiently for him to ingest much? What if it didn't even work? She needed to leave tonight if she was going to have any chance of saving her brother.

"Hey. You okay? You're not going to cry again, are you?"

There was no mistaking the genuine alarm in Colton's voice, and Maddie struggled to push down the guilt she felt at deceiving him. She raised her gaze to his and forced herself to smile.

"Of course not." She gave a shaky laugh. "I'm as well as can be expected, considering tomorrow I'll be thrown into prison, and who knows when they'll let me out?"

He gave her a tolerant look. "They're not going to throw you in jail, Madeleine."

Maddie couldn't help it; her eyes blurred with sudden tears that had nothing to do with acting. "I think they will. I'll lose my job. I'll lose everything." She bent forward and rested her forehead in one hand. "What was I thinking?"

"Hey." Colton's voice was low and warm. Before she quite knew what he was doing, he took her half-empty glass from her hand and set it down beside his own. Then he was tugging her gently into his arms. "Tell me what's going on. Tell me why you were planning to rob the diner. I'm pretty sure any bank would work with you to settle an outstanding debt. So come clean and tell me the truth."

God, he felt so good. His arm was around her shoulders and one hand stroked up and down her bare skin. She was so tempted to just turn to him, wind her arms around him and let his strength seep into her.

With difficulty, she pulled slightly away and blinked

back the tears. "I already told you," she finally murmured. "I'm over my head in debt, and I had a moment of insanity. I wasn't thinking straight. I made a mistake. It won't happen again."

"Damn straight it won't."

Slowly, Maddie raised her gaze. His face was closer than she'd realized. His eyes were so black she could barely distinguish his pupils from the surrounding iris. As she watched, the resolve visible there became something else, something that caused her chest to tighten in anticipation and sent her pulse rocketing. His gaze wandered lower to her mouth.

Maddie stared, fascinated, as his lips slowly descended. He was going to kiss her, and suddenly she wanted to know just how his mouth would feel against her own. She already knew how wonderful his arms felt around her; how would they feel when combined with the intensity of his kiss? Of their own volition, her lips parted and her eyelids drifted closed.

She started when he pushed her gently away and surged to his feet. He strode over to the fireplace and braced one hand on the mantel, his back to her. He raked a hand through his hair and Maddie could sense the tension coiled within him.

"Go to bed, Madeleine," he said over his shoulder. His voice was low and rough.

She rose to her feet and stood uncertainly for a moment. But the rigid set of his shoulders dissuaded her from saying anything. Turning, she made her way into the bedroom.

As she pulled back the bedsheets, she heard Colton

leave the cabin. He was gone for several long moments, and when he returned, Maddie peeked through the doorway to see a black duffel bag slung over his shoulder, and a sleeping bag tucked under his arm. He dropped the bag onto the floor, and Maddie saw the words *U.S. Marshal* emblazoned in yellow along the side.

She quietly closed the door, leaving it slightly ajar so that she could still hear Colton as he moved around in the other room. She got into the bed fully clothed and settled beneath the blanket. It seemed she lay there for hours before the lights in the living room were finally extinguished, although she knew it was only about thirty minutes. How long would it be before the sleeping pills took effect?

She stiffened when the door to the bedroom was silently pushed open. Forcing herself to breathe evenly, Maddie watched from beneath lowered lashes as Colton stood silhouetted in the doorway with the faint light from the fireplace behind him. He stood looking at her for several long minutes, until Maddie was certain he would hear her heart pounding. After what seemed an eternity, he quietly backed out of the room and drew the door closed behind him.

She sat up and pushed her hair back from her face, her breathing uneven. What had he been doing, and why had he felt compelled to check on her? Was he just making sure she hadn't escaped out the window? Or had some other reason warranted his sudden appearance? Was he feeling ill? Did he suspect her of drugging him? Or had he had a change of heart and decided he wanted to finish what they'd almost started out there on the couch?

She knew he found her attractive; she'd seen the expression in his eyes when he'd held her. She'd even considered using sex as a way to coerce him into helping her, but had rejected the idea. Colton Black didn't strike her as the type of man to be easily seduced, and even if he was, she didn't know if she had the courage to go through with it. Just the thought of being with him that way caused her stomach to knot up. He'd make it good for her; she knew that instinctively. But she also knew she'd hate herself afterward. She might not have much, but she still had some self-respect.

Maddie forced herself to lie down again. For the next hour at least, her mind raced with thoughts of what she would do once she left the cabin. She checked the luminous face on her watch. It was nearly midnight. She hadn't heard any sounds from the other room in quite a while.

Cautiously, she sat up and pushed the blankets aside. Her backpack was still in the cab of the truck. At least that was one less thing she had to worry about. Drawing a deep breath, she stood up and stepped cautiously to the door, treading lightly so the floorboards wouldn't creak. Picking up her shoes in one hand, she prepared to creep through the living room in her stocking feet.

She opened the bedroom door and peeked out. The fire was little more than embers now, and the room was in darkness except for one kerosene lamp beside the sofa, turned low. Tiptoeing silently into the room, Maddie peered over the back of the couch.

Her breath caught.

Colton lay sprawled on top of his sleeping bag, one muscled arm bent over his head, his other hand resting on his taut stomach. His shirt had ridden up just a bit, giving Maddie a tantalizing glimpse of burnished skin above the waistband of his boxers. Even in sleep he exuded a raw sexuality that made her mouth go dry. His face was turned to the side, and his lashes lay dark against his chiseled cheekbones. His jaw sported a faint shadow of whiskers, and Maddie had a sudden urge to know how they would feel against her skin. She swallowed hard and found it an effort to pull her thoughts back to her task.

Creeping past the sofa, she crouched next to the duffel bag, biting her lip at the soft rasping sound the zipper made as she pulled it open. Keeping a wary eye on Colton, she rummaged through his gear until she found what she was looking for—a pair of handcuffs. As she drew them quietly from the bag, her fingers brushed against something else; something cold and hard. With her free hand, she pulled out a pistol. It was Colton's service revolver. It felt heavy and unfamiliar in her palm, not at all like the toy gun she had handled thus far. With a grimace of distaste, she dropped it back into the duffel bag. The small noise disturbed Colton, and with a soft groan he flung an arm across his eyes as if to block out the dim light from the nearby lantern.

Maddie held her breath until he relaxed and his own breathing became even again. The ancient sofa was upholstered in a thick, tweedy plaid except for the slatted arms, which were oak. She studied the construction for a moment, trying to estimate the thickness of the wood. Colton's breathing was still deep and steady.

Clutching the handcuffs tightly, Maddie rose silently to her feet and crept to the sofa. She leaned over Colton. His arm still covered his eyes, but his mouth was exposed to her hungry gaze. She couldn't help but stare. It was a luscious mouth, made for sinful pleasures. Her eyes traced the shadowed contours of his jaw and lower, to the strong column of his throat, where his pulse beat steadily.

She told herself it didn't matter if she stared at him; he was asleep and unaware of her perusal. And she was just looking, after all. She had no intention of... touching him. At least not in *that* way. But she would have to touch him if she was going to go through with her plan. With his arm flung across his eyes, it took her only an instant to cinch one handcuff around the strong wrist and lace the other end through the wooden slats of the couch.

She wasn't prepared when he mumbled sleepily and she suddenly found herself staring into slumberous dark eyes. He gazed up at her with a bemused expression and said something incoherent. Before Maddie could guess his intent, he brought his free hand up and slid it under her hair to cup the nape of her neck and draw her down for his kiss.

For a moment, she was too shocked to protest. Then, as his lips moved warmly and sensuously against hers, she gave a moan—whether of protest or pleasure, she wasn't sure. His mouth was hot and sweet, and with a soft sigh of capitulation, she melted against him and allowed herself to respond for one brief, blissful moment. He groaned in satisfaction and drew her closer, slanting his lips across hers and parting them for the intrusion of his tongue.

His kiss was intoxicating; drugging in its effect. For a moment, nothing else mattered except the wild, sweet longing that surged through her veins. He had pulled her down so that she was lying almost fully on top of him, her breasts flattened against the muscled hardness of his chest. He tasted faintly of sweet bourbon, and he smelled like wood smoke and unadulterated male. The combination was devastating to her heightened senses. He shifted restlessly beneath her, and there was no mistaking his growing arousal.

It took every vestige of willpower she had to pull free from that kiss. For a moment they stared at each other, their breathing ragged. The sleepiness in those black eyes had changed to something else; something hot and raw and full of sensual promise.

Before she could change her mind, she reached behind her head and grasped his free hand, lacing her fingers with his.

"Madeleine," he rasped, "I don't think—"

"Shh." She bent down to brush a searing kiss over his lips, and then lingered for several long, tantalizing seconds. She couldn't help herself; the taste and feel of him were irresistible. Then, before he could guess her intent, she pushed his hand over his head and quickly snapped the other handcuff around his free wrist. The chain on the cuffs threaded through the slatted arm of the sofa effectively trapped his hands over his head.

"Hey," he protested with a bemused laugh. "What're you doing?"

"Just a little precaution," Maddie said breathlessly.

Avoiding his heated gaze, she straddled his lean hips and then scooted back on his thighs just enough to free his pelvis from her weight. She had seen him put his truck keys in his front pocket. She glanced swiftly at his face. He was watching her with a half smile, uncertain of her intent. With both his arms raised over his head like that, she couldn't help but notice the impressive bulge of his triceps. She had to fight the urge to slide her hands along the contours of his chest and the undersides of his arms, to fit her hips against his and lean forward until her breasts brushed his chest.

She couldn't look at him as she slid her hand into his pocket, searching for the keys. The hard length of his arousal was evident beneath the denim fabric of his jeans.

"If you're trying to get into my pants, I'm more than happy to oblige." His voice was slow and his words slightly slurred. He made a movement to help her, but was halted by the handcuffs.

"What the—?" He twisted his head and stared in bemusement at his shackled wrists.

Damn. The first pocket was empty. Maddie switched her attention to the other side. Colton jerked at the cuffs, twisting his body sideways in an attempt to wrest his hands free.

"Please, Colton," Maddie begged, struggling to stay seated on his lean body. "You'll only hurt yourself."

He stopped long enough to fix her with a hard glare,

his dark eyes beginning to focus with awareness of what she was doing. "Don't do this, Madeleine." His voice sounded rough, still groggy with sleep. "Uncuff me right this damned minute."

Maddie bit her lip, then swiftly shoved her hand into his other pocket. Colton gave a roar and bucked his hips in an attempt to unseat her. With a cry of alarm, Maddie found herself pitched onto the floor. She scrambled away from the sofa, watching in horror as Colton's violent struggles lifted the piece of furniture clear off the floor.

"It's no use, Colton," she gasped, and opened her hand to reveal the set of keys. "I already have them."

If anything, his struggles became more enraged. Maddie pushed herself to her feet, intent on grabbing her shoes and getting out of there.

"Madeleine," he said, his voice harsh and his eyes burning into hers. "You can't run forever, and there's no place for you to hide. I'll get free, and God help me, I *will* find you."

Maddie paused. He had stopped thrashing, and the fierceness of his gaze almost made her believe him.

"Then I guess I'll be taking this," she said, and bent down to retrieve the gun from his duffel bag. She tried to hold it with a modicum of confidence, but was so repulsed by the cold slickness of it that she might as well have been holding a snake. "Don't try to stop me, Colton. Don't come after me, or you'll force me to do something I'll regret. Just let me go."

"Damn it, Madeleine!" It was obvious that he was struggling to harness his rampant temper. "Please. Just listen to me for a minute. I can help you. But don't do this. Don't go out there by yourself. Stay here, just until morning. We can figure this out together."

She couldn't stay.

She had to get out of there and fast. He was doing it again; using that compelling voice to cement her feet where she stood, listening to him despite her determination not to. If that wasn't enough, the sight of him lying on the sofa with both arms handcuffed over his head was almost too enticing to resist. For one brief, wild instant, her imagination surged. How long would he resist if she decided to take advantage of his position? She wondered how much longer she could resist the temptation to find out.

"I—I'm sorry, Colton. I have to go." She shoved her feet into her shoes and all but ran toward the door, determined not to look at him. With her hand on the broken latch, she paused. "I left the keys to the handcuffs in your duffel bag. I just want to say thanks for everything. I'm sorry, too, that we couldn't have met under different circumstances."

Before he could say anything to make her change her mind, she bolted out of the cabin and pulled the door closed behind her. But as she sprinted toward his truck, she heard his bellow of rage and shivered.

He was right.

She could run, but he'd find her. She only hoped when he did, it wouldn't be too late.

4

COLTON LISTENED TO his pickup truck roar away into the night, and wanted to howl with frustration. Drawing a deep breath, he forced himself to calm down enough to analyze the situation he found himself in. The sofa was pretty sturdy. Still, if he could exert enough pressure on the joint where the armrest met the back, he might be able to break it free.

Ten minutes later, he rolled off the couch and dropped the remnants of splintered wood onto the floor. Staggering over to his duffel bag, he fished through his gear until he came up with the key to the handcuffs, and released himself. He felt dizzy. He felt sick to his stomach. He felt as if he'd been poisoned.

He knew he needed to go after Madeleine, but first he needed to clear his head. He stumbled through the dark bedroom and into the adjoining bathroom. God, he felt wretched. Under the fluorescent light, his normally bronze skin had a sickly hue to it. His mouth tasted like cotton and his head throbbed. Turning on the faucet, he scooped handfuls of cold water onto his face, and then opened the small medicine cabinet in search of something to relieve his headache.

His eyes narrowed as he picked up the small prescription bottle on the first shelf. The cover was missing. There were three capsules inside. Bending down, he tipped the small trash basket toward the light and peered inside. There, at the bottom, lay the crumpled shells of at least five capsules, possibly more.

He couldn't help himself; he leaned weakly over the sink and started to laugh. The little witch had slipped him a Mickey Finn. Luckily for him, the prescription was outdated, otherwise he might find himself in serious trouble and miles from any hospital. At least it explained the misery he was feeling now. But his laughter lasted less than thirty seconds as he considered the ramifications of what Madeleine had done.

She had taken his gun.

Jesus.

The whole situation had just escalated from serious to seriously bad. And all because he'd been duped by a pair of shimmering gold eyes. He groaned at the memory of how he'd reacted to her tears. He'd held her, comforted her. Christ, it had taken every ounce of self-control he had to send her to bed alone. When he'd awakened later to find her bending over him and looking as if she might devour him, he'd assumed she'd wanted to pick up where they'd left off. Kissing her had seemed as natural a response as breathing. He just hadn't been prepared for the effect it'd had on his senses. He'd wanted her. Badly.

Now he couldn't help but wonder how much of her

behavior that night had been genuine, and how much had been an act in preparation for ditching him. It didn't matter now. He had to find her. She had his service revolver. Even if she had no intention of using it, just the fact she had it made her dangerous, and any law enforcement officer would be well within his rights to shoot her if she so much as made a move for the weapon.

He braced his hands on the edge of the sink and groaned, cursing himself. He was a complete idiot. He had allowed his emotions to influence his actions. He'd underestimated her desperation. Even knowing she was in trouble, he hadn't thought she would act so rashly, and had let his guard down. As a deputy marshal, he knew better.

He should never have let Madeleine leave the diner. He should have contacted the local authorities and had her taken into custody right there in Lovelock. Instead, he had violated protocol and bucked every rule in the law book. And now the woman he'd thought to help was out there, armed and dangerous, and more vulnerable than she realized. He had no choice but to contact the authorities and let them know she'd stolen his gun.

He'd lose his badge. At the very least, he could find himself suspended. Ironic, really, since the one thing he'd always prided himself on was that he always got his man. The guys in his district would get a good laugh when they learned he'd been outsmarted by a woman toting a toy gun.

The craziest part of all was that he still felt a compulsion to help her. The urge had nothing to do with her golden good looks, or even with the way she made his body respond to hers. Instead, it had everything to do with the real fear and desperation he had seen in her eyes. She reminded him both of the fox that had been trapped in his cabin and the boy in the courthouse. He hadn't been able to help the kid, but he could help Madeleine. He *needed* to help her.

He rubbed his hands over his face and drew in a deep breath, willing the lingering nausea to subside. This wasn't over yet. His truck was running on fumes, and she didn't know about his reserve tank. He doubted she'd make it back down the mountain before she ran out of gas. If he headed out now, he could still overtake her.

COLTON CAME ACROSS the abandoned pickup truck about three miles down the dirt road beyond the cabin. He checked the cab, but there was no sign of his keys, his gun or her backpack. He fished his flashlight out of the back and examined the area around the vehicle until he picked up Madeleine's footprints. She was heading down the far side of the mountain, and she was running.

She'd been gone less than an hour. Colton estimated she might have made it to one of the secondary roads, but there was no way she could have made it out to the main highway. With luck, he could still catch up with her.

Reaching under the rear fender, he retrieved his spare ignition key. Inside the cab, he flipped a switch for the reserve gas tank, grateful now that he'd invested the extra money for that added feature, and even more grateful that Madeleine hadn't known about it. The engine sprang to life, and he roared down the mountain.

Keeping one eye on the uneven road, he reached over and opened the glove compartment, relieved to see his backup revolver was still there. At least she hadn't discovered that one. He grabbed the handheld radio that was stashed beside the weapon and made a call to the local dispatcher, giving her only the briefest information about what had transpired. Then he waited. Less than five minutes later, his cell phone began to ring. He looked at the caller ID; it was his boss, U.S. Marshal Jason Cooper.

"Deputy Black," the familiar voice growled without preamble, "would you care to tell me what in Sam Hill is going on?"

"Sir, all I'm asking for is twenty-four hours. Just twenty-four hours to bring this girl in. I went willingly with her from the diner, and I've spent the past twelve hours with her. She's not about to hurt anyone, and I'll stake my life on the fact she won't use that gun."

"And if she does? She's already committed a class D felony in taking that weapon, Deputy Black."

"I take full responsibility, sir. But she won't use it."

There was a long silence. Colton respected Jason Cooper, who had a reputation for being unflappable and making sound decisions. Jason and he had worked together for over five years, and Colton considered him a friend, but right now, he couldn't guess which way Cooper's thoughts might be going. He only knew he had to reach Madeleine before Cooper loosed the authorities on her. If Colton didn't find her first, she'd get herself killed. He was sure of it.

"All right." Cooper's voice was low, and Colton could hear the reluctance in it. "I'll put a hold on the APB for the next twenty-four hours, but no longer. I'm only doing this because it's you. If it had been anyone else making this kind of request, the answer would be an unequivocal no. And this doesn't mean you're off the hook—I still want answers. Just remember, if you don't have her in custody within the next twenty-four hours, it's out of your hands."

"I understand, sir. Can you do me a favor and run a background check on her? I need to know what she's involved in."

"Already in progress. I'll have it to you shortly."

"Thank you. She'll be in my custody soon." He hung up the phone and leaned harder on the accelerator.

There was a small gas station at the base of the mountain, just as Madeleine had said. The lights were off, but there was a mobile home on the property behind the station and adjoining general store, and Colton could see a light burning in one of the windows. He needed gas, and he doubted he'd come across another station before his reserve tank went empty.

He parked the truck and pounded on the door of the trailer until it was opened by a white-haired man with a grizzled beard and sharply assessing eyes.

"Where the hell's the fire, son? Whaddya mean by hammering on my door in the middle of the goddamned night?"

Colton withdrew his wallet and held up his badge for

the man to see. "My apologies, sir. I hate to disturb you at this time of night, but I need some gas." He opened his wallet and withdrew twice the amount of money he knew would be required to fill his tanks. "I hope this will compensate you for your trouble."

The old man squinted at the money and then chuckled. "Well, son, I guess that might just make me feel a little less put out."

Colton followed him over to the gas station and waited as the old man turned on the pumps and the overhead lights. He peered at Colton as he inserted the nozzle into the gas tank. "A U.S. marshal, you say? What're you doing out here at this time of night? Tracking down an escaped felon?"

Colton grimaced. "Something like that." He fished in the back pocket of his jeans and withdrew the photos he had pilfered from the cabin. Selecting the most recent one of Madeleine, he held it out to the old man. "Have you ever seen this girl?"

The man took the photo and peered at it, tipped it toward the light and looked closer, before a bark of surprised laughter escaped him. "Well, I'll be goddamned!"

Colton tensed. "You recognize her?"

He chuckled and continued to stare at the photo. "I guess the hell I do. That's Maddie Howe and her son of a bitch, no-good, wastrel grandfather."

"Maddie Howe?"

"That's right. Short for Madeleine, or some such nonsense. 'Course, when she was growing up, we always said her name shoulda been 'Maddie-Howe-are-you-going-to-get-yourself-outta-this-mess?'" He handed the photo back to Colton with a derisive snort. "If that's who you're after, it don't surprise me none. That girl was never nothin' but trouble."

Colton frowned. "How so?"

"Hell, she was a liar and a scam artist from day one. Used those pretty looks of hers to rob folks blind. 'Course, we all knew what she'd been through, so we wasn't gonna turn her over to the law. Figured she'd end up there soon enough on her own, with or without our help." He shook his head. "Guess we was right, after all."

Colton's curiosity was more than just piqued. "What had she been through?"

The old man shrugged. "You name it and that girl's been through it. Lost both her folks early on. She was raised in them hills by her grandpa, but to my mind that weren't no excuse for takin' advantage of people who jes wanted to help her."

Colton's lips tightened. He knew how that felt. "When did you last see her?"

The man sighed and scrunched his face up, considering. "Aw, shoot, I dunno. Maybe ten or twelve years ago. She and her brother were sittin' right here, scamming some tourists out of their money, and they got caught." He gave a gap-toothed grin of recollection. "Last I saw, she was hauling that pretty little backside of hers into the hills, dragging the boy with her and cryin' her heart out." He snorted. "Her tears might've worked on some, but they never fooled me. Not for a damned second."

Privately, Colton had his doubts. Despite the scornful remarks, he wondered if the old man didn't secretly harbor some affection for Madeleine. Colton wouldn't blame him if he did.

The man pulled the gas nozzle out of the tank. "Well, that ought to do it, son. Now, if you don't mind, I'm goin' back to bed. Good luck with your manhunt. If you do see Maddie Howe again, you be sure and tell her old Zeke says hello. But don't forget to add that if she's thinkin' I'll post bail for her, she can damned well think again." He gave a hoot of hoarse laughter and shuffled inside the gas station to turn off the pumps and the lights.

Colton nodded after the man's retreating back. "Yeah. I'll do that. Thanks for your help, Zeke."

He waited until the old man was safely back in his trailer before he climbed into the truck and headed in what he hoped was the direction Madeleine—Maddie, he mentally corrected—had taken. He would find her.

There had never been any question about that.

5

FOURTEEN HOURS LATER, Colton was beginning to think his instincts might have been wrong. He'd been so certain he was on the right track, that he was minutes away from locating Madeleine. He blew out his breath in frustration and turned away from the check-in desk of the seedy motel he'd tracked her to on the outskirts of Reno. It was nearly four in the afternoon and he reluctantly admitted he had no idea where she was.

After he'd stopped for gas at Zeke's place the night before, he'd followed the mountain track down to where it joined the main road, and then concealed his truck in a thick growth of brush and waited. There was a good chance he'd passed Maddie coming down the mountain. She would have seen the headlights of the truck and ducked into the underbrush to hide. But when two hours passed and she didn't appear, he acknowledged that she must have made it to the highway ahead of him. There was no doubt in his mind that she'd hitched a ride.

He'd pulled into the nearest truck stop during a busy breakfast shift and had passed her photo around to the weary truckers tanking up on coffee. He'd let them know the girl was in serious trouble, and if he didn't find her before the local police did, she could end up dead. He'd gotten no response.

It had been the same with the next half-dozen truck stops he'd visited. He was running out of options. He hated to think of Maddie hitching a ride from a stranger in a privately owned vehicle. Truckers at least had a code of honor on the road. Maddie would be safer with any of them than she would be with some nameless creep who just happened to be driving by.

Colton had been sitting in the parking lot of the last truck stop, trying to figure out what to do next when a brute of a man had tapped on his window. It was one of the truckers. He told Colton how one of his buddies had picked up a girl outside of Winnemucca the night before. She'd been headed to Reno. She'd asked the driver to recommend a cheap motel, and he'd given her a name. That was all he knew.

It had been a lucky break. Colton had made it there in under two hours, only to have the promising lead deteriorate into a complete dead end. The Last Chance Motel was cheap, but if Maddie really had been there, it seemed she'd been repulsed by the seediness of the establishment and had moved on. However, just to be certain, he made the manager open every room so he could check for himself that she wasn't there. There had been several female occupants, but none of them had honey-colored hair and eyes. The Last Chance Motel had been his last chance, all right.

He stood near the window in the small lobby and

glanced speculatively up and down the street. This stretch of road was comprised almost exclusively of cheap motels, pawn shops, liquor stores and bond bailments. Colton didn't know what personal demons Maddie needed to settle in Reno, but he did know she was desperate for money. If she was looking for a place to crash, she'd need to find a place that didn't strap her financially. He blew out his breath in frustration. If he had to search every motel on the strip, he'd do it. The dump across the street called the Hold 'Em Inn was as good a place to start as any.

He put his sunglasses on and had his hand on the door when his attention was arrested by activity at the Hold 'Em Inn. One of the guest room doors opened and a woman emerged. Even from a distance, Colton could see she was drop-dead gorgeous. She was slender, but nicely curved in all the right places. She wore a short cocktail dress made of some shimmery gold fabric that plunged low in the front, and her slim feet were encased in a pair of delicate, strappy sandals. Her honey-gold hair had been swept up into a loose bundle of curls at the back of her head, and she carried a tiny, glittering purse in one hand. As Colton stared, openmouthed, a taxi pulled up. She had opened the door and climbed into the backseat before Colton was galvanized into action.

Wrenching the lobby door open, he sprinted across the parking lot to his truck. That was his fugitive who had just morphed from teenage grunge to elegant sophisticate. The transformation might fool some, but not him. He had her in his sights, and this time he wasn't about to let her get away.

He tailed the taxi through the congested downtown Reno traffic, keeping at least six cars between them. When the cab drew up in front of the posh Glittering Gulch Resort & Casino, Colton pulled his truck to the side of the street and waited. He watched through narrowed eyes as Madeleine climbed out of the backseat and then leaned in through the passenger window to hand the driver some bills. The doorman of the exclusive casino all but prostrated himself at her feet as she turned to enter. Colton snorted in disgust as she gave the man a brilliant smile and swept through the enormous doors.

Yep, he'd sure misread her. She'd done a hell of a job putting on the damsel-in-distress act, and he'd fallen for it hook, line and sinker. Oh, he had no doubt she was in some kind of trouble, but she'd demonstrated she was more than capable of taking care of herself.

Colton swiped a weary hand across his eyes. He had no reason to feel so disappointed, but dammit, he'd never felt so completely *used.* It didn't help that he had only himself to blame. If he'd just done his job and taken her into custody at the diner in Lovelock, he wouldn't be sitting here now, remonstrating himself for his stupidity. Or recalling how hot her kisses had been. Or how he had wanted nothing more than to pull her beneath him on that sofa and make her forget about everything but him.

With a low growl of frustration, he pulled up to the entrance of the casino and thrust the truck into Park. He leaped out and dropped the keys into the valet's hands.

"Keep her close by," he muttered. "This won't take me long."

He strode into the casino and paused, letting his eyes adjust to the relative dimness of the interior. Despite the fact it was still early, the place was thronging with people in T-shirts and Bermuda shorts, and above the laughter and noise was the steady hum of slot machines being furiously worked. The rich, dark carpet was offset by the glittering chandeliers and soft, recessed lighting, and the brilliant flash of colors from the slots.

Colton hated casinos. He disliked everything about them, from the glitz and glamour of the decor, to the phony friendliness of the staff, to the greed that motivated both the owners and the patrons. Worse, he hated what gambling inevitably did to the unwary. He'd seen more than his share of good folks completely ruined by the lure of the one-armed bandits or the gaming tables.

Impatient, he scanned the crowd. He spotted the security personnel keeping a close watch on the machines, and beyond that, the pits where the gaming tables were located. Waving away a scantily clad waitress with a tray of drinks, he worked his way through the slot room toward the tables.

The place was cavernous, despite the deliberate effort to make the individual gaming areas cozy. He'd paused, debating whether he'd find Maddie at the craps or the blackjack tables, when some instinct made him look across to the far side of the casino. There was no mistaking her glorious hair or the body sheathed in shimmering gold. She was speaking with one of the security personnel, and even as Colton began to thread his way through the crowd, the man opened a heavy, ornately carved door and waved her through.

Colton reached the door less than a minute later, but before he could push it open, he found his way blocked by a granite slab of a man who put a restraining hand on his arm. Colton's first instinct was to throw the hand off. Instead, he gave the guard a chilling look.

"Is there a problem?" He knew his voice was unfriendly, bordering on rude, but he was too impatient to be polite.

The man removed his hand, but Colton didn't miss how he stepped forward just enough to prevent him from gaining access to the room beyond.

"I'm sorry, sir," the guard said, looking anything but apologetic. "This is a private gaming salon."

"Meaning?"

"Meaning we require our guests to adhere to a certain...standard." His gaze dropped meaningfully to Colton's black T-shirt and jeans. When he met Colton's eyes, his own were courteous but implacable. "However, we do have a boutique here in the casino that carries menswear, sir."

Colton gave a bark of disbelieving laughter and ran a hand over his hair. "Great," he muttered. He could have pulled out his badge and insisted on gaining entry as a U.S. marshal, but the last thing he wanted was to draw attention to himself. He wouldn't risk Madeline making a run for it. With a stifled curse, he spun on his heel and strode away.

Twenty minutes and several hundred dollars later, he returned to the private salon. The henchman guarding that sacred portal gave him a swiftly assessing look, taking in the black dress shirt beneath the black sports jacket, and then stepped back to open the door for him.

Inside the private salon, Colton quickly scanned the opulent room, noting the distinct difference between the clientele here and the touristy gamblers in the outer casino. This was a high-stakes salon, a fact evident in everything from the expensive designer clothing of the customers to the richly luxuriant furnishings. As he strolled through the room, he knew he was being scrutinized, both by the pit bosses and by the hidden cameras that fed the monitors located in the secluded back rooms of the casino.

He accepted a Scotch and soda from an elegant hostess and sipped it leisurely as he made his way from one crowded table to the next, seemingly trying to decide where to throw his money away.

He spotted Madeleine at one of the blackjack tables and nearly choked on his drink. She had a man on either side of her, and while one leaned down to whisper into her ear, the other stroked her shoulder in a manner that could only be called proprietary. For her part, Madeleine was laughing in delight as she flashed each of them coquettish glances and playfully considered her cards.

If Colton hadn't seen the transformation for himself, he'd never have believed her capable of such behavior. There was no trace of a tomboy or damsel in distress in the creature who sat perched at the gaming table, her breasts displayed to full advantage by the plunging neckline of the dress she wore. The short skirt revealed a long expanse of slender thigh, and Colton's fingers tightened around his glass.

She hadn't seen him. He moved away from the table and took a seat at the nearby bar, turning to watch her as she played. She commanded attention. Even the dealer seemed entranced by her throaty laughter and flirtatious looks. A small crowd of people had gathered around the table to watch, and Madeleine played to them like an expert.

Colton also noticed she had a growing pile of chips on the table in front of her, and although she occasionally lost a hand, he realized she was winning significantly more. An hour passed as he watched. Her pile of chips doubled, and she was attracting attention from more than just the patrons. He kept an eye on the security people who had moved closer to the table and were talking in hushed tones as they watched her. If Colton had any doubts about what Madeleine was doing, they were dispelled by the presence of those men.

Madeleine was a card counter.

While that wasn't strictly illegal, the casino retained the right to remove anyone they suspected of gaming the system, and Colton knew Madeleine was in danger of being forcibly escorted out of the high-stakes salon. He also knew they could bring her to one of those hidden back rooms and question her—or do things to her that might not be entirely legal.

Setting his drink down, Colton strolled over to the table and leaned down to speak into her ear. God, she smelled good.

"Game's up, darlin'," he said softly, his breath stirring the tendrils of hair at her temple. "Collect your winnings before the big bad boys over there decide you don't deserve them, and let's go."

She stiffened as he spoke, and although she didn't look at him, he could sense her shock. She hadn't thought he would find her. Or at least not so quickly. She recovered swiftly, though, scooping her chips into her hands and rising gracefully from the table.

"Thank you so much, but I need to leave," she said, smiling sweetly at the dealer as she handed him a valuable chip. "Big brother's found me, so no more fun."

Only Colton knew she meant big brother as in the Feds, rather than any sibling relationship. She ignored the protests and friendly farewells that her departure generated. She spared Colton just one swift glance before she determinedly pushed past him and sailed gracefully toward the private salon's exit door. But Colton had seen the anguish and hostility in that one glance, and knew she was furious with him for interfering. For putting an end to her amazing winning streak.

He fell into step beside her, cupping her elbow in his hand. "The last time I checked," he murmured, "card counting wasn't looked upon favorably by the casinos."

"How did you find me?" she demanded in a low, tight voice.

"Darlin'," he drawled, "there was never any question of my finding you. In fact, it was almost ridiculously easy." He was lying through his teeth, but there was no way he was going to let her know the frustration and anxiety he'd felt at not being able to immediately track her down. "In fact, if I didn't know better, I'd think you actually wanted me to find you."

She made a low sound of irritation, but otherwise ignored him, making her way toward the cashier's cage. Colton estimated she had close to five thousand dollars' worth of chips in her hands. But in the next moment, he saw two of the casino security guards threading their way through the crowds toward them, and he suspected Madeleine might not get the opportunity to cash out.

"C'mon," he muttered, and steered her toward the exit. "I'll come back later with the chips, but right now I think we need to leave."

"No way," she protested, trying to pull free from his grasp. "I'm not leaving here without my money."

"First of all, darlin'," Colton growled in her ear, "you don't have any choice in the matter. You're in the custody of a deputy marshal, and if you'd like me to cuff you and read you your Miranda rights here in front of everyone, I'm happy to oblige. Secondly, if those apes heading in our direction have anything to say about it, you'll be lucky if you leave here with your skin intact, never mind your precious chips."

Madeleine glanced toward the men who were moving toward them with deliberate steps, and she blanched. She clutched her chips tighter, and it didn't escape Colton's notice when she moved perceptibly closer to him. They were making their way past the rows of slot machines, pushing through the crowd of casually attired tourists, and the exit was just steps away when they were stopped.

"Excuse me, ma'am?" A meaty hand descended on Madeleine's shoulder.

She whirled around to face the two men, her expression one of surprise and innocence. Colton turned as well, preparing to pull his badge out and intervene, when Madeleine suddenly tripped. With a startled yelp, she pitched forward, directly into the unsuspecting guards. She flung one arm up, and Colton watched a handful of brightly colored chips fly into the air, spiraling in all directions. The guards turned their eyes to the chips as well, reaching up in an attempt to snag them in midflight. They hit the ground and bounced, rolling madly beneath the feet of astonished tourists, who began scrambling over each other in their haste to scoop up the coveted disks.

Colton found himself shoved sideways, and nearly lost his balance as a heavyset woman on her hands and knees reached for a chip that had landed between his feet. He staggered, and only just managed to regain his balance when he realized he'd lost sight of Madeleine.

The chips and the security guards were all but forgotten as he spun around, searching the crowd. She was nowhere in sight. He turned toward the exit and cursed as he caught a twitch of her shimmering skirt disappearing into the backseat of a taxi before it sped away.

6

HE'D RUINED EVERYTHING.

She still couldn't believe that he'd managed to find her so quickly. She'd been so careful! She was back at the seedy motel where she'd left her belongings, knowing she had just moments to pack her gear and get the hell out of the Hold 'Em Inn before he'd be there. Regardless of the monumental disaster that was quickly becoming her life, she needed to pull herself together. She had to stop crying and start moving.

Maddie swiped at the tears on her cheeks and stepped out of the fragile sandals she was wearing. She struggled to reach the zip on the back of the dress, swearing softly when she failed to catch it with her fingers. It took several minutes, but she finally managed to unzip it, nearly tearing the delicate fabric in her haste. She stepped out of it, wasting valuable seconds as she folded it carefully between sheets of tissue paper before stuffing it into her backpack. She'd spent way too much for the garment, using the precious money from the sale of her car to buy an outfit that would allow her to gain access to the private gaming salon of the Glittering Gulch Casino. And it had all been for nothing. She'd sacrificed almost half her chips in order to escape, and what remained amounted to just over three thousand dollars—not nearly enough to free Jamie.

Angry tears blurred her vision. She snatched the fake diamonds from her earlobes and tossed them into the backpack on top of the dress before throwing the sandals in after them. She straightened and stood for a moment, listening.

She was just reaching for something—anything—to cover herself with, when the door to the motel room exploded inward.

Maddie screamed, despite the fact she knew precisely who it was silhouetted in the doorway. She snatched up a pillow and held it against herself, knowing it did little to conceal the fact she wore nothing but a silk thong.

She stared at Colton in mute despair. He was clearly furious. He slammed the door shut behind him and advanced into the small room. Maddie backed away, hugging the pillow tightly against her bare breasts. Even as her heart leaped in alarm at the dangerous expression on his face, there was another part of her that secretly thrilled at seeing him.

He looked dark and forbidding in his black shirt and jacket. His face was set in taut lines, and his eyes traveled slowly over her, lingering briefly on her damp face, missing nothing. Maddie felt herself flush beneath his cold scrutiny.

"What?" she demanded, taking refuge in sarcasm.

"Your badge gives you the right to barge unannounced into a lady's room?"

"When that *lady* is in possession of a stolen gun, you're damned right it does," he growled. "I want to know what the hell is going on, *Maddie*. Why would a girl like you resort to robbery, kidnapping, drugging, auto theft and cheating at cards? Tell me, please, because I'm not getting it."

He advanced into the room, and Maddie stepped back, not missing his use of her nickname. "At least turn your back and let me get dressed."

He snorted. "No way, darlin'. I'm not letting you out of my sight."

His eyes were cold and challenging as he continued to stare at her, and Maddie knew there was no choice but to get dressed as quickly as possible. With her gaze locked on his, she dropped the pillow and reached swiftly for her jeans. His lips tightened and she thought he swallowed a little convulsively, but otherwise his lean features betrayed nothing at the sight of her nudity.

She struggled into the jeans, leaning forward to yank them up her legs. When his gaze became riveted on her breasts, she snapped upright and without pausing to button her jeans snatched a T-shirt from the bed and dragged it over her head.

"So what now?" she asked waspishly, shoving her bare feet into her sneakers as she fastened her pants. "You drag me to the nearest precinct and throw me in jail?" She shot him an accusing glare. "Isn't it bad enough I lost all my winnings? That was my one chance to make everything right, and you went and ruined it all." Her voice broke.

"That's crap and you know it." His voice was harsh. "You were cheating, and if I hadn't intervened you'd be spread-eagled across a backroom pool table right now, begging those apes at the casino to take the money and just let you go."

He was furious, that much she could tell. It was there in his tightly coiled muscles, his rigid jaw and the way his eyes flashed black fire at her. She shivered.

"I've managed to get along without you for this long; I'd have been okay." Even to her own ears, her tone was less than convincing.

He snorted. "Yeah, right. So where in hell did you learn to count cards, anyway?"

She tipped her chin up and met his gaze squarely. "My father taught me when I was a little girl."

His lips tightened. "That must have been one hell of a childhood. Why do you need so much money? Whatever the reason, it can't be legal."

Maddie swallowed. There was a part of her that wanted to confide in him, to tell him of the fear that consumed her, and what might happen to her brother if she didn't come up with fifty thousand dollars in the next few days. But another part of her feared he could completely destroy her brother's chance for survival if he insisted on intervening. If the kidnappers even suspected she had involved the law, they would kill Jamie.

So instead of answering, she hugged herself around the middle and stared out the window, refusing to look at Colton.

He made a sound of disgust. "C'mon," he finally said, swiping a hand across his eyes. "Let's get out of this dump."

But when he attempted to take her arm, Maddie jerked it away. "Don't touch me."

If he did, she just might lose it. Might fling herself against his broad chest and weep all over his jacket. Now, more than ever, she needed to be strong. She needed to keep her head clear and figure out how to get out of this mess. She needed to get that money and contact the kidnappers, and she needed to do it soon. Time was running out.

She saw Colton's lips tighten in response to her sharp command. With a growl of frustration, he grabbed her backpack off the bed and opened the door to the motel room, ushering her out.

As she slid into the cab of the truck, she watched him cautiously. He started the engine and then looked over at her. Maddie knew her mascara was probably smudged around her eyes from crying, and her hair had come loose from the elegant updo.

"You look tired," he observed curtly. "I'm going to take you someplace where you can have a shower and a decent meal, and then we'll talk." He arched a black eyebrow, as if expecting her to argue.

But Maddie just nodded. She couldn't even summon the energy to fight with him. She was completely exhausted. And hungry. She hadn't eaten anything since the cold ham sandwich she'd shared with Colton the previous night. Right now, a hot shower and a good meal sounded like heaven. After that, there would be time enough to escape.

COLTON WANTED TO throttle her. It was either that or kiss her. He was furious, both with her and with his own attraction to her. Despite the fact he knew her to be a cheat and a liar, he couldn't deny that he wanted her.

Christ.

He couldn't get the image of her standing naked and defiant in the motel room out of his head. Her breasts were perfect, round and firm and tipped with the sweetest pink nipples he'd ever seen. Even in his anger, he hadn't been immune to her. He could still feel her lips moving against his, feel her body, soft and pliant, sprawled over him. She might have had an ulterior motive in kissing him back at the cabin, but even in his drug-induced haze, he'd recognized her desire. She hadn't faked that.

Beside him, she was silent and miserable. She stared out the window, chewing her lower lip. They drove in silence until they reached one of the larger chain hotels in downtown Reno. Colton opted to pay the valet to park his truck in a guarded lot. He still intended to go to his cabin, and couldn't afford to have anyone steal the supplies from the back.

Throwing Maddie's backpack over one shoulder, he took her elbow in one hand and grabbed his duffel bag with the other, then led her into the lobby. As he secured a room, he was acutely aware of her standing at his side, tense and unhappy. When they reached the room, Colton locked the door and switched on the table lamps.

He'd chosen a suite with a small living room and dining area, and now he dumped their gear on the nearby sofa.

"Go take a shower," he said gruffly. "I'll order room service."

Without looking at him, she walked into the bedroom and closed the door decisively behind her. Colton waited until he heard the water running in the bathroom, and then ordered dinner for each of them. He peeled his jacket off and draped it over the back of the sofa. As he did so, his eyes fell on Maddie's backpack. Without hesitation, he unzipped it and searched through the contents until he found his revolver. Checking the magazine, he was reassured to see all seven bullets still in the chamber. He placed the weapon in his duffel bag and returned his attention to the backpack.

He rummaged once more through the contents, pushing aside the shoes and clothing until he found a small pocketbook at the bottom. Snooping through Maddie's personal belongings wasn't something he enjoyed doing, but he hoped he might find a clue as to her actions.

Opening her pocketbook, he withdrew her wallet. A lipstick and a hairbrush lay at the bottom of the bag, along with a slim silver holder for business cards. Extracting one, Colton read the words *Certified Public Accountant* beneath her name. She was an accountant? He found the idea both astonishing and amusing. The role of tomboy and femme fatale suited her better than a bean counter.

He replaced the card and tipped the pocketbook toward the light, seeing a slip of folded paper at the bottom of the bag. Pulling it out, he quickly scanned the message written there: "Bring the money or bury your brother."

Colton didn't feel surprised or shocked. Instead, he felt relief. Replacing the contents of her purse, he carefully rearranged her backpack the way she had left it, and moved toward the windows to stare unseeingly at the strip below. At least now he knew what Madeleine's motives were.

Someone was using her brother to extort money from her.

That, he could handle. He didn't know how he would have felt if he'd discovered she was into drugs, or if she was some kind of career criminal. Bad enough that she'd drugged him and stolen his truck and service pistol.

While he didn't know precisely who was threatening her, he knew what kind of people they were. He knew there was an ongoing investigation, in both Reno and Las Vegas, into a rackets ring that involved gambling, loan-sharking and extortion.

Pulling out his cell phone, he punched in the number for Jason Cooper. His boss answered on the first ring.

"Tell me you have her, Black."

"I have her."

"Good," Cooper replied. "Take her over to the Reno sheriff's office. They'll handle it from there."

Colton was silent, and after a long moment, he heard Cooper make a sound of irritation. "Is there a problem, Deputy Black?"

"There's something bigger going on here, sir. I found evidence that her brother is being held for ransom." He glanced toward the bedroom door. "What if the Canterinos are behind this?"

The Canterino family ran a crime ring that extended all the way to New York City, with several factions in Las Vegas, Reno and even Costa Rica. The ring was suspected of issuing usurious loans at prearranged rates of interest, amounting to 175 percent. Collection of the unlawful debts was sometimes accomplished by removing a body part, usually a finger or an ear. Unfortunately, the victims were unwilling to talk to law enforcement, knowing that they might lose their lives if the Canterino henchmen found out.

"My instincts tell me this girl is into something bad, and we need to let it play out. This could be our opportunity to get some solid evidence on the Canterino family and their factions," Colton continued.

"I ran a check on Ms. Howe," Cooper replied, "and while she came up clean, the same can't be said about her family. She comes from a long line of career gamblers and scam artists. It wouldn't surprise me if her brother did borrow money from the Canterinos. He has a rap sheet for underage and illegal gambling. Bring her in, and I promise you she'll talk."

The underlying threat was unmistakable, but Colton knew better. Cooper might come across as a hard-ass, but Colton had known the other man for a long time, and knew he'd never harm Madeleine.

"If I bring her in to the sheriff's office now, she's going to close up tighter than a minister's daughter," he said, keeping his voice low. "I think we need to let this play out and find out who the extortionists are.

My bet is she'll lead us right to the Canterinos. Her brother stands a better chance of escaping with all his body parts intact if we intervene. But if we don't take this opportunity, there are going to be more victims."

"Send me everything you have. I'll contact Deputy Burns in the Reno district and get something set up. I'll be in touch."

After clicking off, Colton glanced toward the bedroom. The water was no longer running in the bathroom. Thinking about Madeleine alone with any of the Canterino gang made his blood run cold. If her brother had made the mistake of borrowing money from them, his life was in danger. And Madeleine likely had no idea just how ruthless those men could be.

He could help her, keep her safe. Was he still seriously pissed off over the way she'd used him? Oh, yeah. But the thought of what had driven her to such desperate measures pissed him off even more.

He turned at the sound of the bedroom door opening. With her wet hair combed slickly back from her face, Madeleine stood there wearing a white terry cloth bathrobe that was several sizes too big for her. She had a fresh, just-scrubbed look that made her look young and innocent, although Colton knew better. She gave him a wary glance as she advanced into the room.

"So what now?" she asked.

Colton didn't miss how she kept the sofa between them. His frustration rose a notch, but he was prevented from responding by a knock on the door.

"That'll be room service," he said grimly. "Which means now we eat."

He opened the door to the hotel waiter and paused long enough to sign the tab before pulling the rolling cart into the room and closing the door. Maddie sat down and watched as Colton uncovered the dishes and placed them on the table. Not knowing what she would like, he'd ordered them each a large steak with a baked potato and salad.

"Eat up," he said, sitting across from her.

She dug into her meal with unconcealed energy, and for a moment Colton just watched her. She glanced up at him, and as if realizing her lack of manners, put her fork down with a self-conscious grimace.

"I'm sorry," she said. "I guess I was hungrier than I realized."

"Don't apologize." Colton picked up his own fork and knife and sliced off a tender bite of steak. "I like to see a woman who isn't afraid to enjoy a meal. Go on, eat."

Maddie watched him for a moment, and then picked up her utensils. They ate in silence after that, although Colton knew she was aware of him. It was there in the way her gaze would flit across the table to him, but never reach his face. For his part, he was uncomfortably aware of her. Several times, she adjusted the front of her robe when it threatened to gape open, allowing him brief glimpses of the smooth skin beneath. Knowing that she was likely naked under the terry cloth made it almost impossible for him to concentrate on his meal, never mind enjoy it.

Finally, when she had finished, she pushed her plate away and sat back in contentment, oblivious to how the robe slid open over her legs, revealing the slender length of her thighs.

"Delicious," she declared with a smile.

Colton pushed abruptly back from the table and gathered up their plates, depositing them unceremoniously onto the cart. When he turned back, Madeleine was eyeing him warily. Her hair had begun to dry, curling in soft, honeyed waves around her face. More than anything, Colton wanted to unfasten the sash that held the bathrobe closed, push aside the terry fabric and slide his hands over her satiny skin. He wanted to feel her beneath his palms, hear her breathing change as he aroused her, watch her eyes darken with desire. Disturbed by his own lustful thoughts and needing to do something—anything—to distract himself, he abruptly confronted her.

"Who's extorting money from you?"

Her hazel eyes widened in alarm, before she quickly schooled her features and assumed an air of confusion. "What are you talking about?"

"It's a simple question, Madeleine. Who is threatening to hurt your brother unless you bring them money?"

With a gasp, she sprang to her feet. Her eyes flicked to her backpack, still on the table near the door. "You went through my things." Her voice shook with disbelief and anger. "How dare you."

"Did your brother take money from a loan shark, Madeleine?"

Her eyes snapped back to his, flashing with anger and indignation. "You had no right to search my stuff."

"I asked you a question. Who has your brother?"

"That's none of your business. I can take care of it if you would just *let me*."

Her stance was defensive, every muscle poised to either fight him or flee. Colton had never felt such frustration in his life. He wanted to help her, but there was a part of him that also wanted to hurt her, just a little, for the hell she'd put him through. For making him want her so much.

Her breathing was coming faster, and her breasts rose and fell in agitation beneath the terry cloth. The sash had loosened, and he could see the sweet fullness of one breast, almost completely exposed where the fabric had slipped to the side.

"Really?" he asked, his voice full of derision. "You can take care of it? How much do they want, Madeleine, and how are you going to pay them? We both know you have very little money." Knowing he was a crude bastard for even insinuating it, he gestured toward her bare breast. "Or maybe you're planning on providing some other means of payment?"

Eyes flashing, Maddie took a swing at him, intent on slapping his face, but Colton easily caught her wrist in one hand.

For an instant, they stood staring at each other. The air between them crackled with energy. Her cheeks were flushed and her eyes stormy as she glared at him. Her robe still gaped open, her breasts rising and falling swiftly with her agitation. Colton was barely holding his frustration in check, but when her gaze shifted to his mouth, something inside him finally snapped. He recalled again the feel of her on top of him, kissing him, and with a low growl of defeat, he hauled her against his chest and crushed his mouth over hers.

She stiffened for a fraction of a second, and then was kissing him back with an urgency that shocked him, even as it released the pent-up lust and frustration he'd been feeling since the incident in the cabin. Maddie's hands were everywhere, smoothing over his shoulders and his back, cupping the nape of his neck as she angled her face for a better fit. The sensation of her tongue against his only ratcheted up his need for her. With the last vestiges of his control, he pulled back long enough to bracket her face in his hands and search her eyes.

"Madeleine—"

"Please." She placed her fingers over his mouth. "Don't talk. Just kiss me. I know you want this."

He did. More than he'd wanted anything in a long time. Even knowing he was taking advantage of the situation—of her—he couldn't prevent himself from lowering his head and claiming her mouth again. But he was unprepared when she made a soft sound of approval and her fingers moved to the buttons of his shirt, tearing at them in her urgency.

"Maddie, sweetheart," he said against her lips, "we don't need to rush this."

"I do," she said, her breath coming in warm pants as she pressed moist kisses against his face and neck. "You're so hot. I don't want to wait."

She'd unbuttoned his shirt and dragged the tails from his waistband, pushing the fabric aside to slide her hands over his heated skin.

Colton groaned and thrust his fingers into her damp

hair, deepening the kiss. Her fingers moved to the fastening of his pants, and the brush of her knuckles against his bare stomach made him catch his breath.

"Darlin'—"

"Please," she whispered against his lips, her voice urgent. "I want you now."

Colton was a goner. "You can have me," he promised between kisses. "I just want you to trust me."

"I do, I do," she assured him breathlessly, drawing down his zipper and skimming her hand over the waistband of his boxers.

Colton dragged his mouth along the side of her neck, lingering on the soft spot at the base of her throat where her pulse beat frantically. "You don't ever need to run from me," he said in a low, fierce voice. "I'll never hurt you."

Maddie made an inarticulate sound of agreement and slid her hand inside his pants. She cupped him through the thin fabric of his briefs, and Colton groaned at the sensation. He pushed her robe off one shoulder and pressed fevered kisses against her smooth skin, inhaling her scent. She smelled fragrant and sweet.

"You're so beautiful," he muttered between kisses. "Let me help you."

"It's okay." She angled her head to give him better access, even as she curled her fingers around his length. Her voice sounded husky in his ear. "I'll pay my pound of flesh, to you or the blackmailers, if it means getting my brother back."

Colton recoiled.

Her words were like a dousing of frigid water on his

rising lust. Slowly, he reached down and wrapped his fingers around her wrist, pulling her hand away from where he was still hard for her. Grasping her by both forearms, he leaned back and searched her eyes. Maddie tossed her hair and glared back at him, defiant. She made no move to cover herself where the bathrobe had slid from her shoulder, fully exposing one perfect breast. Her lips were slightly parted, and her breathing came unevenly as she watched him.

Colton stared at her in disbelief. He couldn't believe she thought he was using her; couldn't believe that she'd try to use *him* in such a crude way.

"Jesus," he finally said, and thrust her away from him. "You think I'm using you? If that's what you believe, then you don't know the first thing about me."

"Well, you don't know the first thing about *me,*" she retorted, "and I want to keep it that way!"

Colton grabbed her by one arm and dragged the terry cloth robe over her exposed body. "Lady," he growled, "with just one phone call, I can find out every detail of your life, from the grades you got in middle school to when you first got laid."

Maddie flushed, but tipped her chin up. Her voice trembled just the tiniest bit. "Maybe that's true, but you still won't know *me.*"

With sudden clarity, Colton realized he wanted to know her. He wanted to know how she had gotten herself into such a desperate situation. He wanted to know everything about her, from her greatest fear to her wildest fantasy. But most of all, he wanted her to trust him. There was something about her that drew him; something that went beyond her curvy figure and smoking-hot kisses. He liked her courage and her determination to help her brother. This was a woman who would do anything to protect her loved ones. Her loyalty and resourcefulness was something he admired, especially considering her upbringing. She'd overcome so much adversity and had so much promise. He didn't want anyone to destroy that.

He blew out a breath, feeling suddenly weary, and swiped a hand across his eyes. "Look, it's getting late and we should both get some sleep."

"Fine." She bit the word out before she spun on her heel and stomped toward the bedroom. She was through the door before Colton realized her intent, but as she furiously tried to slam the door in his face, his booted foot was already there.

"Oh, no, sweetheart," he said, smiling into her outraged eyes. "There is no freaking way I'm letting you out of my sight. In fact, just to be sure you don't pull another disappearing act..." He held up his hand, where a pair of handcuffs dangled from the end of one finger—the same handcuffs she'd used on him the previous night.

Maddie gasped. "You wouldn't."

"Oh, I most definitely would," he said in a silken voice.

With his foot still wedged in the door, he peeled the black shirt from his body and dropped it onto the floor. When he pushed the door open and kicked his shoes off, she tried to retreat, but Colton caught her again by the arm. Only when he'd snapped one end of the handcuffs around her wrist and the other end around his own did she understand.

"Oh, no!" she protested, trying unsuccessfully to jerk her arm away. "What if I need to use the bathroom during the night?"

"I'm a light sleeper, and I don't mind keeping you company," he said smoothly. "I'll even promise not to watch."

"This is outrageous," she hissed.

"Is it? You didn't think it was outrageous last night, when you shackled me to the couch." With his free hand, Colton removed his wallet and placed the handcuff key inside. "C'mon, let's get some sleep. I don't know about you, but I haven't slept in two days."

To her credit, she looked guilty. "Look, I'm sorry I drugged you, and I'm sorry I took your truck, but now you understand how desperate I was, maybe you can forgive me." She gave him a trembling smile. "You really can trust me. I won't try anything, I promise."

Colton snorted in disbelief and walked her over to the bed. "Sorry, darlin', but I'm not buying it. I don't trust you one bit."

He pulled back the blankets on the bed, and still wearing his unzipped jeans and socks, eased himself down onto the mattress. With their hands bound together, Maddie had no choice but to do the same. She yanked the sash of the bathrobe tight around her waist and giving him a disgruntled look, gingerly lay down, putting as much space as possible between them.

Leaning over, Colton dropped his wallet onto the floor beside the bed where Maddie would have no chance of reaching it without crawling over him and waking him up. Without another word, he dragged the blankets over both of them and then snapped off the bedside light. They lay side by side in the darkness, but Colton was acutely aware of their linked wrists.

"Just don't forget I'm tethered to you. Don't roll away from me in the night," she said darkly. "I have no desire to wake up draped across your body."

Colton didn't answer, but the images her words evoked ensured that he lay awake for several long hours. He listened to her breathing and knew the precise instant when she finally drifted into sleep and her body relaxed beside him. Her fingers brushed against his where they were shackled together, and as if subconsciously seeking more contact, she rolled toward him until he could feel her warm breath against his bare shoulder, feel the heat that rolled off her beneath the covers. With a groan, he flung his free arm over his eyes, knowing it was going to be a long night.

7

MADDIE OPENED HER eyes to utter blackness, momentarily disoriented. She was surrounded by warmth, and something thumped steadily beneath her ear. Slowly, she became aware that she lay with her head on Colton's bare chest, with her free arm flung across his torso and their manacled hands entwined between their bodies. His breathing was deep and even, and Maddie lay completely still for a moment, listening to his heartbeat and savoring the sensation of being pressed against him. If he woke up, he'd probably shove her away, and as much as she hated to admit it, she liked their current position.

She felt safe.

She recalled again how turned on she'd been when he'd kissed her in the living room. Maybe she'd deliberately set out to seduce him in order to gain the upper hand, but she'd quickly found herself overwhelmed by his sheer potency. The guy knew how to kiss, and when she'd curled her fingers around his straining erection, she'd forgotten everything else. The only thing she'd been able to think about was how much she wanted him.

She'd tried to get him to stop talking, but honorable to the end, he'd kept insisting that she needed to trust him. Maddie didn't want him involved in the blackmailing scheme, didn't want to drag him into the mess that was her life. She just wanted to lose herself in him, however briefly, and forget about everything else but the pleasure they could give each other. Had she planned to use him? Oh, yeah, but not in the way that he'd believed.

He slept deeply, and as Maddie's eyes adjusted to the dark, she could just make out his features. He'd turned his face toward her, and his chin rested against her hair. At some point, they'd pushed the blankets down, and Maddie could see her own hand, pale where it rested against his ribs. Except for the trail of dark hair that extended from his navel to beneath the waistband of his pants, his skin was smooth and tawny, his nipples dark, flat disks on his tautly muscled chest. Cautiously, she smoothed her fingertips over one small nub, watching in fascination as it puckered beneath her touch.

Colton's breathing didn't change, and emboldened, she let her fingers drift over his skin, enjoying the warmth and texture. He stirred and muttered something, but didn't wake up.

Maddie wanted him awake. She wanted to feel the energy and strength that he radiated, and wanted it focused on her. She had never met a man like Colton Black before.

Honorable.

Capable.

Sexy as hell.

And once this nightmare was over, she'd be unlikely

to ever meet anyone remotely like him again in her life. Sure, he was gorgeous, but that wasn't the only thing about him that she found attractive. She recalled again how kind he had been to her at the cabin, and how safe he'd made her feel when he'd held her. And how had she repaid him? By drugging him and shackling him to a sofa with his own handcuffs, and then stealing his truck. The guy probably hadn't had a decent vacation in years, and she'd gone and completely ruined his time off.

But she could make it up to him now. She told herself she was doing it for him, but there was a part of her that acknowledged she *wanted* to have sex with Colton Black. She needed to know how it would feel to be surrounded by his warmth and passion; to have him inside her and watch his face as he lost control. She couldn't deny that she was doing it for herself, too. It had been so long since she'd been with anyone who had made her feel the way Colton did—alive.

Slowly, she pressed her mouth against his chest and slid her free hand along his torso, feeling the ridges of muscle beneath her fingertips. He sighed in his sleep and then stretched languorously, like a big cat. Maddie shifted closer, smoothing her palm over his skin as she planted soft, moist kisses against his chest. His breathing changed, became sharper. Lifting her head, she saw him watching her through glittering eyes.

Their wrists were still linked, their arms pressed close where they rested between their bodies. Raising herself on one elbow, Maddie slowly bent her head and covered his mouth with her own, softly pressing her tongue past his lips until she encountered the hot slide of his. For a moment he lay perfectly still as she worked her mouth sensuously against his. Then he groaned loudly and raised his free hand, only to bury it in her hair and hold her head in place as he returned her kiss with heated intensity.

Maddie was unprepared when he rolled over her, turning her onto her back beneath him. He linked his fingers with hers where they were joined by the handcuffs, and then pushed her hand over her head. He loomed over her in the darkness, and Maddie was aware of a sharp excitement, anticipating what would come next.

"Darlin'," he rasped, his voice husky with sleep, "what are you doing?"

She cupped his jaw, rubbing her fingertips over his whisker-rough skin. "What do you think I'm doing? Please, Colton..." She emphasized her words by shifting restlessly beneath him, pushing her hips against his in a way that he couldn't mistake.

"This is crazy," he muttered, just before he dipped his head and claimed her mouth in a kiss so carnal that Maddie felt her insides turn to liquid.

She clung to him, wrapping her free arm around his neck and pushing her fingers through his hair, even as she pulled her knees back to cradle him more completely between her thighs. Beneath the terry robe, she was almost nude, and with an impatient sweep of his hand, Colton parted the fabric and cupped one breast in his big palm. Maddie gasped into his mouth at the intimate contact. His hand was warm and callused, and when he rubbed his thumb over her nipple, she felt an answering throb of sensation between her legs.

Colton dragged his mouth from hers and skated his lips along the side of her neck, causing her to shiver beneath his sensual attention. She clutched him tighter.

"Please," she whispered against his hair.

"Soon, darlin'." His voice was a husky rasp. He dipped his head to draw one nipple into his mouth. The slick heat of his tongue was almost more than Maddie could take, and she heard herself whimper even as she held his head in place, rubbing her fingers against his scalp. He used his free hand to cup that breast as he flicked his tongue over the tight bud of her other nipple, before drawing it into his mouth in turn and sucking sharply.

Maddie shifted restlessly beneath him. The hard ridge of his erection pressed against her, and she pushed back experimentally. The movement caused him to rub directly against her, and she grunted softly at the contact. Her heartbeat throbbed in every limb, but most strongly where his aroused flesh met hers.

She tightened her knees against his ribs and subtly urged him closer with her heels at the back of his thighs. To her dismay, he eased his way down her body, dragging the blankets with him, and pressed his mouth against her bare skin as he went. Maddie's breath came in fitful pants, her breasts and stomach quivering beneath his touch. But when he moved his hands to her knees and firmly pushed them outward, she stopped breathing altogether.

"Colton…"

"Shh." His warm breath fanned against the fragile barrier of her panties. "Let me."

Raising her head, Maddie looked down the length of her body at him. He was a large, dark shape between her pale thighs. His hands still cupped her knees. Maddie curled her fingers around his wrist where they were manacled together, but whether to stop him or urge him on, she couldn't say. As she watched, he slid his palms down the inside of her legs, dragging her hand with his, and gently eased her thighs farther apart. Tugging the silk panties to one side, he used his thumbs to stroke her. Flames ignited beneath his touch, and Maddie knew she was slick with arousal. As she watched, he dipped his head and licked her once. Her head fell back against the pillows, and she groaned loudly.

"Do you like that?"

Locked in a paralysis of pleasure, Maddie could only manage to squeeze her fingers around his. But when he pressed his tongue against her clitoris, she nearly came off the bed. He swirled his tongue softly over her, causing her to writhe helplessly beneath him. He knew her body better than she did, using his mouth to torment her, even as he slid one finger deep inside her. Maddie's muscles contracted around him, and her hips moved as he began to thrust rhythmically into her. But when he flicked his tongue hard against the swollen rise of her flesh, Maddie began to come undone.

"I'm not going to last," she managed to say, her voice sounding strangled. She clutched his wrist in warning, but when he eased a second finger inside her, she cried out as powerful contractions racked her and pleasure crashed over her, more intense than anything she had ever experienced before. She didn't think she could stand much more and survive, but Colton didn't stop until he'd wrung every last tremor from her quivering body.

Maddie pushed weakly at his head with her free hand, and he released her. But instead of settling himself between her legs to finish what he had started, he pulled himself up alongside her and lay down on his back, their linked arms between them. She sensed rather than saw him fling his free arm over his face. In the darkness, the only sound was their uneven breathing. She knew he was still aroused; had felt the hard thrust of his erection as he'd climbed away from her. When he didn't turn toward her, or give any indication that he wanted to continue, Maddie rose on her elbow.

Despite the amazing orgasm he'd given her, she still wanted him. Wanted to feel him inside her, and to give him the same incredible release that he'd just given her.

Tentatively, she touched his shoulder. "Colton—"

"Go to sleep, Madeleine." His voice was rough and he sounded weary.

For a moment he lay still, and then she felt him reach over the edge of the bed with his free hand and retrieve his wallet from where he had left it on the floor. In the next instant, he freed himself from the handcuff, only to snap the loose end around the narrow slat of the headboard. Maddie didn't even have time to protest before Colton rose to his feet and crossed to the bathroom. He was silhouetted briefly in the doorway when he snapped on the light, and then he shut the door firmly behind him, leaving her alone in the dark.

Tentatively, she tugged at the restraint, but there was no way she was getting herself free. The knowledge that he didn't trust her stung, although she acknowledged that she hadn't given him any reason to. Already, he knew her pretty well, because given the chance, she definitely would have ditched him again. Even at this time of night, she would have slipped away in order to find her brother.

The shower turned on, and she could imagine Colton stripping down and standing beneath the steaming spray of water, still aroused, and no doubt angry because of it. Her body still thrummed where he had touched her, and she recalled again the feel of his hands and lips on her skin. He'd wanted her; she was positive about that. So why had he stopped? Did he think he was abusing his authority as a U.S. marshal, or was there a part of him that found her repugnant?

The sound of running water stopped, and several moments later the bathroom door opened. In the brief seconds before he snapped off the light, Maddie saw him clearly, and let out a deep breath. He wore nothing but a towel wrapped around his lean hips, and steam wreathed his impressive body. Then he shut the light off and walked toward the bed. Leaning over, he captured her wrist in one hand, and Maddie felt him fitting the key into the handcuffs. Droplets of water fell from his hair and plopped onto her bare skin. He smelled clean and fragrant, and his warm breath fanned her cheek as he released her.

Straightening, he stood by the side of the bed for a moment, and Maddie wondered how much of her he could see. She dragged the edges of her bathrobe together, self-conscious in spite of the darkness.

"I'll be in the other room," he said, his voice low. "Don't even think about trying to sneak out, because I won't be asleep."

Without waiting for a response, he left the bedroom, closing the door firmly behind him. Maddie rubbed her wrist where the handcuff had been, and then dragged the blankets over her. Curling onto her side, she listened as he moved around in the adjoining room. She felt small and miserable And even knowing that she shouldn't get involved with Colton Black for a hundred different reasons, she felt shunned.

Rejected.

She bunched the pillow beneath her cheek. Colton might make her feel safe, but now she wondered if it was only an illusion. He said that she could trust him, but she knew better. She couldn't trust anyone. She'd learned from bitter experience that she could rely only on herself. But for the first time she could recall, the knowledge made her feel desolate.

IN THE LIVING room, Colton dug through his duffel bag and dragged out a clean set of clothes, dropping his towel to pull on the boxers and jeans. Despite the shower, he was still aroused and aching.

Barefoot and shirtless, he sat down on the sofa and scrubbed his hands over his face, knowing he was out of his league. It had taken all his willpower to leave

Madeleine alone in the bed and not make love to her fully. More than anything, he'd wanted to bury himself in her sweet body, but he'd be damned if he'd let her accuse him of using her. When he finally made love to Madeleine—and he would—it'd happen when there were no more secrets between them. He needed her to trust him unconditionally.

Blowing out a hard breath, he rose to his feet and retrieved his smartphone from where he had left it on the table. Scrolling through the messages, he saw that Jason Cooper had sent him the background report on Madeleine. Opening the document, he quickly scanned the contents.

Her mother had died of cancer when Maddie was just ten years old, leaving her and her two-year-old brother in the custody of their father, a compulsive gambler. James Howe had had a police record, mostly public disturbances related to his losses at the casinos. He'd been banned from most of the major gaming establishments in both Reno and Las Vegas, and his death seventeen years ago had been ruled a suicide. Madeleine would have been twelve years old at the time. Following his death, Madeleine's grandfather had gained custody of the children, raising them in the cabin in the hills.

But Gramps had his own problems with gambling and alcohol, although it seemed he'd made an effort to clean up his act once his grandchildren had moved in with him. Somehow, he'd ensured that Madeleine went to college, and had established a small trust fund for her brother's education. But a lifetime of excess had eventually taken its toll, and he had died of liver failure in an Elko nursing home two years ago.

Colton closed the document and set the phone aside. Opening his wallet, he withdrew the photo he'd taken from the cabin—the one of Madeleine and her brother sitting on the steps there. He tried to imagine what it must have been like for her, losing both her parents at such a young age, and having to live with an old man who gambled and drank too much. How had old Zeke described him? As a wastrel. Not exactly a model guardian for two children. Colton could well believe that Madeleine had resorted to conning tourists out of their money; she'd probably had no other choice if she wanted to take care of her younger brother.

Colton thought of his two younger half brothers, both of them in their teens. He'd never had to worry about either of them, secure in the knowledge that they were well loved and cared for. Despite the fact his own parents had never married, Colton hadn't doubted either of his parents' love.

He'd had an unorthodox upbringing, to say the least. His father had been a student at Stanford University, and had spent one summer working on a Shoshone reservation near Paradise Valley, where he had become involved with a young Shoshone woman. Their brief affair ended when Colton's father returned to California, but by then his mother had been pregnant. Colton's dad had wanted to get married, but his mom had been more pragmatic, insisting they would be happier apart. She'd been right, and despite the fact they hadn't married, they'd remained close.

So Colton had grown up in what he considered to be the best of two worlds. He'd spent the school year living with his father in Monterey, and his summers on the reservation with his mother. When he was eight years old, she had married a rancher and moved to Pyramid Lake, about three hours north of Reno, where they had started their own family. But they'd never made Colton feel like an outsider, and he felt equally comfortable in his mother's rustic ranch house as he did in his father's sprawling seaside villa.

He also had two best friends—Aiden Cross, his childhood buddy from Monterey, who now served as a navy SEAL, and Siyota Fast Horse, a patrolman on the reservation. Colton found it ironic that both he and Siyota had chosen careers in law enforcement, considering they'd done nothing but raise hell as kids.

With a deep sigh, he stretched out on the sofa and bunched a throw pillow behind his head. The air-conditioning was cool against his still-heated skin, and he welcomed it. He thought of Madeleine in the other room, and how she had felt in his arms.

How she had tasted.

He recalled again the sweet sounds she'd made as he'd used his hands and mouth to bring her to orgasm. Just the memory of those noises made him groan in frustration. He was beyond exhausted, but knew he wouldn't sleep.

He needed to develop a plan to free Madeleine's brother, without putting her in danger. Reaching into his pocket, he pulled out the small key that he'd retrieved from the tin box at the cabin and studied it closely. He'd seen enough similar keys to know it went to a safety deposit box. He could only imagine what Maddie's grandfather might have kept locked away. She hadn't given the key a second glance as she'd sorted through the items in the tin box, so he knew her grandfather hadn't shared the information with her. As Colton slipped the key back into his pocket, he decided part of his plan would include finding the bank and deposit box that this key belonged to.

He knew Cooper would help him, and his friend Aiden had just returned from Afghanistan for three weeks of rest and relaxation before he needed to report to duty in San Diego. As a navy SEAL, he had some seriously bad-ass skill in hostage rescues. Both men were in California, and could be in Reno within a matter of hours. But as a plan slowly began to formulate in his head, Colton knew he would need more manpower than just himself and two other guys.

He'd need a tribe.

8

"WHERE ARE WE GOING?"

Colton didn't so much as glance at Maddie, instead keeping his focus trained on the dark highway ahead. "Somewhere safe."

He had woken her up early that morning by turning on the bedside lamps and telling her brusquely that he wanted to be on the road in thirty minutes. He'd retreated into the living room before she was fully awake.

Maddie had been wrenched by anxiety as she'd quickly dressed. Would he mention the previous night? Did he regret what they had done? Did she have the courage to face him? But when she'd finally ventured into the living room, he'd occupied himself by packing his duffel bag, gesturing toward her breakfast on the table. She'd glanced at his discarded dishes. From all appearances, he hadn't had much of an appetite.

Maddie had picked at her omelet and fruit, and had gulped down two cups of strong coffee before Colton abruptly told her they were leaving. She felt more than a little intimidated by his attitude, and self-conscious enough that she couldn't quite bring herself to meet his eyes. But he was so cool and remote, she thought she might have imagined what had happened the previous night if she hadn't known better.

But while they could avoid talking about it, the knowledge of what they had done hung in the air between them. It was there in the set of his shoulders and the way he deliberately avoided any physical contact with her. She decided she was fine with that, but every time she glanced at him, she was reminded of how his hands had felt on her body, and a little shiver went through her.

Outside, it was still dark, and Madeleine had at first been afraid he was taking her to the authorities. But he'd left the city and turned onto Highway 80 again. She had tried to figure out where he was taking her, but the best she could determine was that they were headed north.

Away from Reno.

Away from her brother.

"I don't need for you to take care of me," she said quietly. "I can do this without you, but only if you leave me in Reno. I need to be in Reno."

He spared her one swift, hard glance. "Is that where he's being held? Your brother?"

She hesitated, not wanting to tell him anything. Her greatest fear was that the law would somehow become involved, and the kidnappers would kill Jamie rather than risk being caught.

"Madeleine, right now I'm your best chance at saving your brother." Impatience edged Colton's voice, making it sound harder.

"You could get him killed."

"Not if you tell me everything." He glanced over at her. "Together, we can get your brother back, but you need to talk to me, Madeleine."

Maddie turned to stare blindly out the window. He was doing it again, lulling her into believing that she could trust him. But she had no reason to mistrust him, not after all he had done, and especially considering the horrible things she'd put him through. And he still hadn't dragged her to the nearest sheriff's station.

Then there was last night. She would willingly have had sex with him. She'd wanted him badly, even after he'd brought her to orgasm, but his entire focus had been on her pleasure, and he'd taken none for himself. After he'd left, she'd felt rejected, but now she wondered if perhaps he'd retreated out of some sense of honor.

"Okay, let's start with what *I* know," he suggested quietly. "Your brother's name is Jamie. You were both raised by your grandfather in that cabin. You went to college in Elko, and at some point during that time, your brother came to live with you, and he finished high school there. Now he's a senior at the California Institute of Technology, and like you, he's something of a math whiz. A real genius, by all accounts, and his specialty is counting cards. My guess is that he's gotten himself involved with some bad moneylenders. If they're who I think they are, Jamie's life is in real danger."

Maddie turned to stare at Colton. He'd said that with one call he could find out everything about her, but the knowledge that he'd actually done so was disconcerting.

"What else did you find out?" she asked waspishly.

A ghost of a smile touched his mouth. "Relax. I have no idea when you first got laid, if that's what you're wondering." He was silent for a moment, and Maddie could see a muscle working in his lean jaw. "About last night—"

"Forget it." Her voice came out sharper than she intended. "I already have."

He slanted her a swiftly assessing look. "Really?"

"Yes." She sounded defiant.

"I haven't forgotten." He watched her with heated eyes. His voice dropped an octave. "I haven't forgotten one damned thing. In fact, it's all I've thought about since I left you last night."

"So why did you leave?" As soon as the words left her mouth, Maddie regretted them. They made her sound pathetic.

Needy.

"Madeleine—"

"Forget it," she said again bitterly. "I don't care. The only thing I care about is getting my brother back safely."

"I want the same thing," he insisted. "That's why you need to tell me what you know about these men. How did your brother become involved with them?"

Maddie was silent for several moments, weighing her options, before she blew out a hard breath. "Do you remember I told you that my father taught me how to play blackjack and poker?"

Colton gave a brief nod.

"Well, my grandfather taught Jamie. He taught both

of us how to do more than just play. He showed us how to game the system." She turned again to stare out at the dark landscape. "I was good at it, but Jamie was really good. He got himself in trouble a couple of times during high school, buying into private games and then cleaning out players who were twice his age, and ten times meaner. The last time he did that, he ended up in the hospital. When he left for college, I made him promise to give up gambling."

"But he didn't."

Maddie snorted. "If you discovered anything about my background, you know that addiction runs in my family like a virus. Addiction to alcohol, gambling, the thrill of the game. Call it whatever you want. My brother has it in spades, just like my father and my grandfather."

Colton surprised her by reaching across the seat and covering her hand with his own, gently squeezing her fingers. "We'll get him back."

Maddie drew in a trembling breath and nodded, not trusting herself to speak. What Colton didn't understand was that Jamie was all she had left. Sure, he'd been in trouble before, but never anything like this.

"Do you know if he was with anyone else when he came to Reno?"

Maddie shook her head. "I don't know. He belonged to a group of blackjack players at school. I think he traveled with them, but I can't be sure." She gave Colton a brief smile. "He knew I disapproved, so he never talked about it."

"But you knew he was still gambling?"

"I didn't know for sure, but I suspected. The last

time I visited him at school, I was shocked by the expensive things he had. You don't afford brand name clothing and top of the line electronics on a college work-study salary."

"Tell me how you learned he was in trouble."

"Someone delivered a funeral arrangement to my house the other morning, along with a note." She shivered. "A few hours later, I got a phone call from Jamie. He wasn't actually crying, but I could tell he was close to it, and that he was afraid. Really afraid. I think they were hurting him."

"What did he say?"

"That he was sorry. That he'd had a bad run of cards and had lost some money. He'd given the men my name, and told them I was good for the amount he'd lost."

"How much?"

"Fifty thousand dollars."

Colton swore softly. "How long did they give you?"

"Seventy-two hours. Which is why we need to go back to Reno. We've already burned almost forty-eight of those hours. If I don't bring the money to the drop area by tomorrow morning, they'll kill Jamie."

"Did he give you any information about the men who were holding him?"

"No. They only let me talk to him for a few seconds."

"Do you have an address for the drop site?"

Maddie shook her head. "No. They gave me a phone number and told me to call it tomorrow morning at ten o'clock."

"Do you have the number?"

She gave him a tolerant look. "Of course I do."

"Okay. Tomorrow morning, you can make the call, but there's no way you're going to the drop site."

"Colton—"

"Trust me," he said grimly. "Nobody is going to hurt your brother."

They drove in silence after that until the sun began to lighten the edges of the sky, washing the horizon in streaks of pale gold and orange and casting the mountain peaks in stark silhouette.

"Where are we going?" Maddie ventured. They had left the highway and were winding their way steadily through the foothills of the Sierra Nevadas.

"Pyramid Lake."

Even as he said the words, they passed a road sign. Maddie read the words as they swept past, and then swiveled in her seat to stare at Colton in disbelief. "You're taking me to an *Indian reservation?* Why?"

He spared her one hard glance. "I grew up on Pyramid Lake."

"You're Paiute?"

"Shoshone. At least, on my mother's side."

Maddie shook her head. "I still don't understand. Why are we here?"

"Because I have a plan, and I need you to be safe while I'm gone. And the safest place I know is here, with my family."

Electrified, she stared at him. "Gone? What do you mean, *gone?*"

He compressed his lips. "I have a plan to get your brother back, but I need you to stay here."

"Whatever your plan is, I'm coming with you. They'll be expecting to see me, not a U.S. marshal."

"You're out of your league, Madeleine. I know the kind of men your brother is involved with, and I don't want you anywhere near them. This is bigger than you realize. If I'm right, the men who have your brother run an illegal gambling ring that extends from coast to coast, and even outside the U.S. borders. They're professionals. Besides, what are you going to bring? You have no money."

"No thanks to you," she retorted, on the verge of tears. "If you hadn't gotten involved, I'd have won enough money from the casinos to pay his debt, and my brother would already be home."

Colton made a scoffing sound. "That's bull and you know it. First of all, there's no way you could have won that much money without the casino figuring out what you were up to. Second of all, if I hadn't gotten involved, you'd be dead or in jail. Not to mention if you hadn't flashed that gun back at the diner, I wouldn't have had to get involved at all. You got me into this, and now you have to live with it."

"He's all I have." She hadn't meant to blurt out the words that had been drumming through her head since this nightmare had begun. But if anything happened to Jamie, she didn't know what she would do. He was all she had left in the world, and she was terrified that he would be injured or worse.

To her surprise, Colton pulled the truck to the side of the road and thrust it into Park. Reaching across the seat, he hauled her into his arms.

"I know what he means to you." His voice was gruff against her ear. "I promise you I won't let anything happen to him. I have a plan, but it means leaving you for a short time. I won't be gone long, but I need to know you'll be safe—that you won't do anything stupid." Pulling back, he bracketed her face in his hands and searched her eyes. "Okay?"

Maddie stared at him, her throat tight with emotion, and managed a brief nod. His expression relaxed fractionally, and his gaze drifted over her features. She could see the concern that lingered in his dark eyes and the lines of tension around his mouth, and guilt stabbed at her. If not for her, he'd be enjoying his fishing vacation.

"I'm sorry," she said, her voice catching. "I never meant to get you involved. You've done so much for me, and all I've done in return is lie to you, steal from you, drug you...."

To her surprise, Colton grinned. "Hey, every relationship has its problems."

Maddie stared at him, too surprised by his irreverence to immediately respond.

"Look," he said softly, stroking his thumb across her cheek, "try not to worry so much. This is what I do best, okay?"

"Colton—" She broke off, unsure how to continue. She was unaccustomed to revealing her feelings, and wasn't certain Colton would want to hear about them, even if she could find the words.

"What is it, darlin'?"

His thumb still moved sensuously against her cheek,

and his expression was so warm that Maddie felt her heart turn over in her chest.

"I lied." She swallowed hard. "I haven't stopped thinking about last night, either."

Colton's expression softened, and he drew her toward him. "Ah, Madeleine..."

"No, don't be nice to me," she begged. "I don't deserve your kindness."

He smiled again, a tender curving of his lips as he drew her inexorably closer. "No," he agreed. "You deserve much more."

His mouth came over hers in a kiss so sweet that Maddie felt tears prick the back of her eyelids. He coaxed a response from her, pushing past her lips to taste the inside of her mouth, his tongue teasing hers. Maddie sighed in pleasure, acknowledging that this was what she had been wanting.

All too soon, Colton pulled back. "We should get going," he said. "We don't have a lot of time."

She nodded and watched as he paused with one hand on the shift. He angled his head to look at her.

"I know what your brother means to you, Madeleine. I have two brothers of my own, and I'd do anything for either of them." He paused again, as if considering his words. "But I want you to know that you're not alone in this. You have me now."

He pulled onto the road, and Maddie settled back into her seat. Her mouth still tingled where he had kissed her, and she could still feel his hands on her, as if his touch had been imprinted on her skin.

She knew he was sincere in wanting to help her, but while she might have him now, she knew she wouldn't have him for long.

9

KISSING MADELEINE HAD been a mistake, but Colton couldn't bring himself to feel sorry about it. Her reluctant admission that she couldn't stop thinking about last night had given him a fierce sense of satisfaction, but her belief that she didn't deserve kindness bothered him. Her sweet response to his kiss made him want to take her to bed and show her just how much she deserved, but he hadn't been kidding when he'd told her they didn't have much time.

Now he drove past the sign that signaled their entry onto Pyramid Lake Indian Reservation. He hadn't visited his mother or brothers in over seven months, and the familiar landscape brought a stab of nostalgia. At a fork in the road, Colton ignored the sign that directed travelers to the visitors center and tribal headquarters, and instead turned down a narrow, deeply rutted road that bisected the nearby prairie. Sensing Madeleine's curiosity, he slanted her a reassuring smile.

"My mother and stepfather have a ranch about two miles down this road."

"What kind of ranch?"

"Cattle. It's a small operation, with about five hundred head, but it provides jobs for some of the local guys."

"What about your father? Where is he?"

"My dad lives in Monterey. He and my mom were never married, but they're still good friends."

"Really?" Maddie couldn't keep the disbelief out of her voice.

Colton grinned. "Really."

She didn't know what to expect, but not the neat ranch house surrounded by a half-dozen outbuildings and a series of paddocks and corrals. The house itself was sprawling, with an enormous wraparound porch, and Maddie could see it was well maintained. Beyond the main house was a large barn, and she could make out the shadowy figures of several people inside. Several older trucks were parked beside the building, and Colton drew his own pickup alongside and turned off the engine.

"Are you okay?"

Maddie dragged her gaze away from the main house, where a woman had come outside to stand on the porch. "I'm a little nervous, I guess."

Colton grinned. "Don't be. We haven't stolen any white women in decades, and the only person likely to go on the warpath is my mother if we track mud through her house."

Maddie flushed. "That's not why I'm nervous."

She hadn't actually given his Native American heritage much thought beyond an appreciation of how it had contributed to his dark good looks. No, it was the thought of meeting his family that made her palms go damp. She barely remembered her own mother, and her memories of her father were all mixed up with vague emotions of anger and fear. Even her grandfather, whom she had loved, hadn't been someone she could look up to or depend upon.

But she sensed that Colton's family was close. It was there in his tone when he talked about them, and she could almost see his body posture change now that he was home. Since she'd met him, he'd been on high alert. Now he seemed marginally more relaxed.

Reaching across the seat, he tucked a strand of hair behind her ear and let his knuckles linger for a few seconds against her jaw. "There's nothing to be nervous about, Madeleine. Come inside and meet my family. Then we'll make plans. Okay?"

She nodded, resisting the urge to turn her face into his hand. Seemingly satisfied, Colton got out of the truck and came around to her side to open the door. She was grateful for his protective bulk as they made their way across the dusty yard to the house. As they walked, several men came out of the barn, while another group appeared from one of the outbuildings beyond the ranch. Maddie was unaware that she had slid her hand into Colton's until she felt the warm strength of his fingers close around hers.

They reached the porch at the same time as the two groups of men. They were all Native American, all around Colton's age, except for one who was older by at least twenty years. He wore his long, dark hair in a neat ponytail beneath his cowboy hat. He strode up to Colton and embraced him, saying something in a language Maddie didn't understand.

Colton returned the man's hug before pulling away and turning toward the woman who stood watching quietly. This was Colton's mother, Maddie knew. She had the same dark eyes, the same watchful manner as her son, and she was strikingly attractive.

"Mom." He pulled her into his arms and gave her a brief hug. "Thanks for having us on such short notice."

"This is still your home. You know that."

Colton stepped away to draw Maddie forward. "This is Madeleine Howe, a friend of mine."

When Colton's mother reached out and took her hands, Maddie could feel calluses on the other woman's fingers. "I'm Susan Waite. Welcome to the Black Creek Ranch." Her eyes were warm as she assessed her.

Maddie gave her an uncertain smile. "Thank you."

Colton drew her attention to the older man. "This is my stepfather, Billy Waite, and these other men are my friends." He turned to his mother. "Aiden Cross is on his way. He should be here within the hour."

Maddie smiled at the men, but their names were a blur as Colton introduced her. The only one she really remembered was Siyota Fast Horse, distinctive because of his name and the Bureau of Indian Affairs police badge he wore on his uniform.

"Come inside," Susan invited when the introductions were over. "I just made a fresh pot of coffee."

"The boys and I are going to head over to the bunkhouse," Colton said. "But Maddie could probably use a cup of coffee." Seeing her alarmed expression, he bent his head close to hers. "I won't be gone long. You'll be fine."

Maddie watched them stride across the yard before reluctantly turning to follow Colton's mother into the house.

"Have a seat," Susan urged her, gesturing toward an enormous farmhouse table in the middle of a large kitchen. "How do you like your coffee?"

"Light, please." Maddie sat down, and as Susan poured coffee for them, she took stock of her surroundings. The ranch house was spacious and decorated in a Southwestern style. It was rustic without being primitive, and the warm tones of the fabrics and textures made Maddie feel comfortable. An open hutch stood against a nearby wall, displaying a collection of handthrown pottery. An assortment of framed photos on the lower shelf caught Maddie's attention, and she stood up to get a better look.

"Is this Colton?" she asked, picking up one photo and tipping it toward the light. Two little boys stood with their skinny arms flung around each other's shoulders, grinning impishly into the camera. Both had shiny black hair and dark eyes, but one boy had deep dimples that Maddie instantly recognized.

Susan came to stand beside Maddie, and handed her a steaming mug of coffee. "That's Colton and his best friend, Siyota, when they were ten years old." She smiled fondly. "They were such little hellions."

Maddie replaced the photo and picked up another one of two different boys. "Who are these?"

"Those are my younger sons, Shane and Wes. They're older now, of course."

Maddie stared more closely at the picture, seeing the resemblance to Colton. "They're beautiful boys."

Susan tipped her head, listening. "I think I hear them waking up."

"They're here?" Maddie couldn't contain her surprise.

"Of course. They might think they're grown men, ready to leave their father's house, but they are still just seventeen and fifteen years old. Normally, they would already be up and helping their dad, but with so many of Colton's friends here, Billy decided to let the boys sleep, and the men did the chores for them."

As if on cue, a teenaged boy shuffled into the kitchen, still rumpled from sleep and looking a bit grumpy.

"Why did you let me sleep so late? What's going on?" He caught sight of Maddie and stopped short, running a self-conscious hand over his short hair. "Sorry, I didn't know we had company."

"Shane, this is Maddie Howe. She's a friend of Colton's."

At her words, the boy's face brightened. "He's here? Where is he? Why didn't you tell me?"

"He's in the bunkhouse with your father, but I think they're talking business—"

But it was too late. Shane disappeared the way he had come, shouting for his brother to wake up. "Colton's here! Hurry up!"

They heard the slam of the front screen door, and Maddie caught a blur of movement through the living room as Wes sprinted after his older brother, hastily pulling a shirt on over his head as he ran.

Susan gave a philosophical shrug. "They adore Colton. He was already a teenager when they were born, and by the time they started school, he was in college. His visits are always a treat for them."

"I have a brother who's not much older than Shane," Maddie told her. "He's always been the most important person in my life."

"But maybe there is room in your heart for another person?"

Maddie threw the older woman a startled look. "What do you mean?"

"I see the way Colton looks at you."

"Oh, no," she said with a surprised laugh. "You're mistaken. I hardly know Colton, and I'm the last woman he wants to get involved with."

Susan studied her over the rim of her coffee cup. "Something tells me he is already involved. He's a good man. The best."

They were prevented from further discussion as Shane and Wes came back into the kitchen, looking disgruntled.

"Colton told us to get lost," Wes said moodily, throwing Maddie an assessing look. "They're planning something, and they won't tell us what it is."

"He said that? To get lost?" Maddie couldn't keep the surprise out of her voice.

"No. He told us to give them twenty minutes and then he'd come up to the house," Shane clarified, pouring himself a cup of coffee. "His friend Aiden just arrived. You know, the navy SEAL. What's going on, Mom?"

"Sit down and I'll make you both some breakfast," Susan said, turning to the enormous stove. "And say hello to Colton's friend Madeleine. She'll be staying with us for a day or two."

Maddie bit back the denial that sprang to her lips, and instead gave each of the boys a brief smile. They sat down at the table across from her, openly studying her. She tried not to stare back, but it was difficult. They were handsome boys, with shrewd dark eyes and gorgeous bone structure, and Maddie could see the promise of the striking men they would soon become. There was a strong family resemblance to Colton, but where he was broad and muscular, the boys were whipcord thin and wiry.

Maddie watched as Susan prepared eggs and bacon, and wondered what was keeping Colton so long. She'd go crazy if she had to sit there for another minute, she finally decided. Pushing her chair back, she stood.

"I'm going to see what's keeping Colton," she announced.

Shane shook his head and gave her a lopsided grin. "I wouldn't do that if I were you. They looked pretty serious, and if Colton wouldn't let me stay, there's no way he's going to let *you* hang around."

Maddie glanced at the youth, affronted. "Why? Because I'm a woman?"

"No," he promptly replied. "Because it looks like they're planning some kind of covert military operation. Colton never lets anyone get involved with official business."

Anxiety washed over Maddie. What was he planning? Didn't he realize that if they tried to intervene in any way, they could jeopardize Jamie's life?

"This isn't official business," she said firmly. "This is personal."

Striding across the kitchen, she opened the door to the porch and nearly collided with Colton coming in. He caught her by the upper arms, steadying her. "Whoa, where are you going?"

"To find out what you're planning," she muttered. "Colton—"

Pulling the door shut behind her, he drew her onto the porch and down the steps. "I was just coming to get you. We need you down at the bunkhouse."

"What are you planning? Shane said it looked like a military operation."

He gave her a sidelong glance. "I want you to call the men who are holding your brother and tell them you need more time."

"What if they refuse?"

"Then we'll try negotiating. The longer you can keep them on the line, the better."

Maddie followed him across the yard to the farthest outbuilding, a rough-planked structure with a corrugated tin roof and windows that pushed out from the bottom. Opening the door, Colton led her into a living room, where at least a dozen men stood around a long table, talking in low tones. They looked up as the two of them entered.

One of the men detached himself from the group and crossed the room toward them. There was something so confident in his manner that Maddie felt her anxiety level drop a notch or two.

"You must be Madeleine."

She nodded, momentarily unable to find her tongue. Up close, the guy wasn't just attractive, he was off-the-charts gorgeous, with a shock of sun-streaked blond hair and the brightest, bluest eyes she'd ever seen. He gave her a reassuring smile, and Maddie felt certain he knew exactly the effect he had on women. As casually as if they'd known each other for years, he slid an arm across her shoulders and drew her slightly away from Colton. He was warm, and Maddie could actually smell him—a mixture of masculine deodorant and soap, and a subtle coconut fragrance that reminded her of sun-baked days on the beach.

"I'm Aiden Cross," he said, dipping his head toward hers. "Did Colton explain what we need you to do?"

Maddie glanced at Colton, the perfect foil for Aiden's fair good looks. Was it her imagination, or did he seem a little bigger and darker than usual?

"Um, yes. He said he wanted me to call the men who are holding my brother, and tell them that I need a little more time to bring them the money they want."

"That's right." Aiden's voice was warmly approving as he smiled into her eyes, and Maddie felt her insides go a little weak. "We have no idea where these guys are holding your brother. They could be anywhere. But once you place the call, we'll be able to pinpoint their location."

She frowned. "But won't we know their location when they tell me where to bring the money?"

"Sure, but we're going to insert our men around the site tonight. That way, they'll already be in place when you deliver the money."

"But what if they change the location at the last minute? There's no guarantee that they won't move my brother during the night."

"The phone call will tell us where they are right now, and let us move in. We'll put a tracer on the signal, and they won't be able to do anything without us knowing their every move."

Her dismay must have shown on her face, because Colton stepped forward and physically removed Aiden's arm from her shoulders, frowning at the other man. "Okay, there's no need to bore Madeleine with the details." He switched his attention to her. "All you need to know is that we're going to get your brother back."

"You're going to send men in ahead of time? Don't you realize you could ruin everything?" Maddie's voice rose a little with her increasing agitation. "They specifically said that if I involve the police, they'll kill Jamie. Why would you send men in?"

Colton tipped his head and looked directly into her eyes. "I think I know who has your brother, Madeleine, and I do know how dangerous they are. Did he ever mention the Canterino family to you?"

She shook her head. "No. I've never heard of them. Do they have Jamie?"

"Once we pinpoint where he's being held, we'll be able to confirm who has him. But this is typical of how the Canterino family operates. They've been under investigation for over a year, but we've never had solid proof of their crimes until now." Correctly interpreting her troubled expression, he dipped his head and again looked into her eyes. "You need to let us handle it. It's what we do."

Before she could protest, Aiden thrust a phone at her. "Call the number you were given and tell them you're in Reno. Tell them you want to come right now and give them the money."

Maddie threw a bemused glance at Colton. "But I don't have it. What if they call my bluff?"

Aiden gave her a humorless smile. "They won't. They'll want to stick to the plan, and this will give us a chance to pinpoint their exact location."

Colton gave her a curt nod, confirming what Aiden had said.

Reaching out, Madeleine took the phone. Aiden turned away, and for the first time, she noticed a metal container about the size of a shoe box sitting on the table. The device was topped by a metal plate that held a series of small lights and toggle switches. The box was connected to a laptop, and Maddie could see a map displayed on the screen.

"What is that?" she asked, looking at Colton.

"It's called a stingray. It works by mimicking a cell phone tower, and getting a cell phone to connect to it. The operator can send a signal to that phone and locate it."

"And you think that will tell you where the kidnappers are?"

Colton glanced toward the table, where Aiden and the men were watching her expectantly. "We've used it before. It works."

"Okay, then." Withdrawing the slip of paper from her pocket, Maddie unfolded it and slowly punched in the numbers. She watched Colton's face as she listened to the phone ring on the other end. He listened as well, using an earpiece attached to the phone she was using.

"Yeah?"

The voice was deep. Abrupt. She took a breath. "It's Madeleine Howe. I was told to call this number when I arrived in Reno."

"I know who the fuck this is," the man at the other end answered. "And you weren't told to call this number when you reached Reno, bitch—you were told to call at ten o'clock tomorrow morning."

The voice was cold and angry, and Maddie felt an answering anger surface from somewhere deep inside her.

"I don't care what you told me," she practically growled. "I'm here now, and I want my brother. Do you understand me? Tell me where to bring the money."

"I'll tell you tomorrow at ten o'clock, and if you don't want your brother returned to you in small pieces, you won't call this number again before then. You understand *that,* bitch?"

"How do I know Jamie's okay? Put him on the phone right now or you get nothing."

The silence stretched, until all she could hear was the whooshing sound of her own blood in her ears. She was vaguely aware of Colton and the other men watching her closely.

"Maddie?"

Jamie's voice, sounding high and frightened, came over the line.

"Jamie!" She clutched the phone closer, her heart nearly exploding out of her chest with fear and anxiety. "Are you okay?"

But it wasn't her brother who answered. It was the first man. "Tomorrow," he snarled. "Ten o'clock."

The line went dead.

Maddie stood listening for several seconds longer, before she finally lowered the phone. "Jamie's alive."

Colton took the phone from her and pulled her toward him for a swift, hard hug. "Of course he's alive. They're not going to kill him, Madeleine."

When he stepped away from her, Maddie immediately missed his warmth and strength. She wanted his arms around her, wanted to hear his voice telling her that everything would be okay. But he was already bending over the table, studying the laptop screen with the other men.

"We have a location," Aiden said, indicating the map. "Here, just north of Reno. There's an abandoned mining operation. I'm bringing up the satellite images now. They should provide a detailed view of the site."

"I'll contact Cooper and let him know where to position his team," Colton said. He looked at the others standing at the table. "We'll leave within the hour. Aiden, you come with me. Siyota, you take your men and follow us."

Maddie watched as they began writing down coordinates and discussing the layout of the abandoned mine. She turned to Colton. "What about me?"

"You'll stay here." When she would have protested, he pulled her toward the door. "We'll be back before dinner. This is strictly a reconnaissance mission, and to put men in place, if need be. But nobody is going in, guns blazing, on these guys, okay?"

Maddie considered him through narrowed eyes. "You promise?"

"Absolutely." Seeing her skeptical expression, he heaved an irritated sigh and drew her outside. "I told you to trust me on this, Madeleine. We have some things we need to do to prepare for tomorrow morning and ensure we get your brother back safely. Because as soon as those bastards realize you don't have their fifty thousand dollars, things are going to get ugly fast."

"But you're not going to do anything today, right?"

"Nothing that anyone will be aware of. But for now, I need you stay here and promise you won't do anything stupid, like leave."

Maddie bristled. "I won't—"

"So help me God, Madeleine, I will handcuff you to the wall if I think you might try to leave this ranch." His voice was a low growl, and she took an involuntary step back. "Promise me right now."

"Okay," she finally agreed. "I promise."

"I'll be back before dark." Without warning, Colton pressed a hard kiss to her mouth before releasing her. "Go back up to the house, and—" he shook his head, looking frustrated "—try to behave yourself."

10

MADDIE HAD THOUGHT the day would drag by as she waited for Colton to return, but Susan had clearly anticipated this. Almost from the moment the men left, she kept Maddie busy, first helping to feed the stable of horses that the ranch maintained, and then by helping to prepare the midday meal for the horde of ranch hands.

Accustomed to cooking for her brother, Maddie had thought nobody could eat more than a teenaged boy. But she hadn't counted on the hungry men who swarmed Susan's kitchen just after noon. Together, she and Susan had prepared an enormous batch of spicy rice and beans and cornbread, accompanied by thick slabs of ham.

The ranch hands made short work of devouring the food, and then quickly went back to their chores, leaving the women to clean up.

Maddie's gaze continually drifted to the window, searching the dirt drive that wound toward the main road, but there was no sign of Colton.

"If he said he'll be back before dinner, then he will

be," Susan said, accurately reading her thoughts. "Why don't you help me with supper?"

Maddie turned and looked at the other woman in astonishment. "Supper? But we've barely cleared away the lunch dishes."

"There'll be even more mouths to feed tonight," she promised. "Colton's favorite meal is my roasted chicken with biscuits and gravy, so that's what we'll have. If you go through that door, you'll find the pantry and the walk-in cooler. We'll need six of the thawed chickens and twenty pounds of potatoes."

Maddie felt her mouth open before she firmly snapped it shut. She'd had no idea the amount of effort involved in running a working ranch, just in feeding the hands. Colton had said this was a small operation, with just over five hundred cattle, but Susan told her there were always fences to repair and irrigation pipes to monitor, and a dozen other tasks related to keeping the animals and machinery in top condition.

By the time the two of them had finished preparing dinner and setting the massive farmhouse table, the sun was beginning to sink over the horizon. Maddie didn't know how much longer she could contain her impatience without taking action.

"They'll be back soon," Susan soothed, sensing her mood. "Try to relax."

"Relax?" Maddie gave a short laugh as she used a spatula to remove hot biscuits from a pan and place them into a basket. "I'm not sure I can." She angled a look at the older woman. "How do you know they'll be back soon?"

"Because I know my son. He's a man of his word." Colton's mom smiled. "And because I saw their headlights turn off the main road about five minutes ago."

Sure enough, as Maddie spun eagerly toward the window, she saw three vehicles approaching the house. They pulled to a halt just beyond the barn, out of her sight. Several minutes later, Colton opened the door, and he and his stepfather and stepped into the kitchen. Colton dumped his duffel bag and a backpack on a chair in the corner as his gaze found Maddie's.

"Okay?" he asked.

She nodded, unable to prevent the rush of pleasure and relief she felt at seeing him again. Despite the large kitchen and oversize table, he made the room seem small with his sheer presence.

"We made supper," she said unnecessarily, indicating the platters of food.

He came forward to snag a biscuit from a basket on the table, biting into it with relish.

"What's in the backpack?" Maddie asked.

"Nothing much. Just some things I picked up for tomorrow."

She wanted to ask more questions, but at that moment ranch hands started entering the kitchen, shuffling past her with mumbled greetings, to take their seats at the table. Shane and Wes appeared from the adjoining room, and Maddie helped Susan finish putting the food on the table.

"We'll talk after dinner," Colton said in a low voice before pulling her down into a chair next to him.

She nodded. "Okay. Where are your friends?"

He slanted her a sidelong look, and his tone was dry and sardonic. "Which ones?"

"Never mind."

"Aiden and Siyota stayed in Reno. Relax," he said, correctly interpreting her anxious expression. "They're just laying some groundwork. Nothing will happen until tomorrow."

Dinner was an energetic event, with so many hungry men at the table, but Maddie noted how both Susan and her husband treated the ranch hands like family. Colton's mom asked after wives and children, and seemed to know the personal issues of each of the men. Even after the meal was finished, nobody seemed inclined to leave the table. Only after they had gone through several pots of coffee and endless war stories about life on the ranch did the men finally stand up and say their good-nights.

Susan turned to Colton. "You and Madeleine can stay in the back wing tonight. I made the bed up this morning, and there are fresh towels in the bathroom."

Maddie looked questioningly at Colton, but he squeezed her hand beneath the table, warning her to silence.

"Thanks," he replied. "I hope you don't mind if we turn in early. It's been a long day, and neither of us got much sleep last night."

Maddie didn't miss the knowing look that Susan exchanged with her husband, but when she spoke, her voice was warm. "I understand." She turned to her sons, who were still sitting at the table, reluctant to leave while Colton and Maddie were still there. "Boys, you have evening chores to do, so why don't you get to it?"

Maddie hid a smile as they groaned in unison. They sounded so much like Jamie had whenever she'd nagged him to do his homework or clean his room.

"Go on," Susan urged. "You can see your brother tomorrow."

Maddie murmured her own good-nights as the boys fist-bumped with him and reluctantly left the kitchen. Colton stood up and retrieved his duffel bag and backpack before drawing Maddie to her feet.

"Thanks for dinner, Mom. It was great."

"I'll see you in the morning, son."

Colton paused. "Actually, I plan on getting an early start, but Madeleine will stay here, if you don't mind."

Maddie would have protested, but he shot her a warning look, causing her to clamp her mouth shut. She wouldn't argue with him in front of his mother and stepfather, but there was absolutely no way he was leaving her behind. After saying good-night, she followed him through the house, her back stiff. On the far side, Colton opened a door to a large bedroom with a cozy sitting area in one corner and an adjoining bathroom. Another door led outside, providing a private entrance to the small apartment.

"This room was used as a separate living area for the cook before my parents took over the ranch," he explained, setting his gear on a chair. "The single men sleep in the bunkhouse—at least the ones who don't live locally."

"And what about you?" Maddie walked across the

room to the window and stood staring out into the darkness, acutely aware of him standing there. "Where do you usually sleep when you're here?"

Colton was silent for a long minute. She watched his reflection in the dark glass as he approached her and then stopped several feet behind her. "I usually sleep in my old bedroom, across the hall from Shane and Wes," he said quietly. "Would you prefer I sleep there?"

Maddie felt her breath catch. His words siphoned up decadent images of him—of them—from the previous night. The rational part of her said he should go sleep in his old room. He was too much of a temptation, and nothing good could come of getting physically involved with him, even if it didn't mean anything. But if he stayed in the main part of the house, she wouldn't know when he left. At least if they were together in the same room, she'd be able to prevent him from leaving her behind. Drawing in a fortifying breath, she turned to him.

"Colton—"

"Forget it," he said, interrupting her. He spun away, rubbing a hand over the back of his neck. "I didn't mean to put you on the spot. I'll sleep somewhere else."

Maddie was silent for a moment. "I was going to say that I'd prefer you to stay here with me. I mean, I'd like for you to stay. I want you to."

His head swiveled, and she found herself impaled by his dark gaze. He studied her for a moment and then nodded. "Okay. Fine. But it's still early. Why don't we sit outside for a bit?"

Without waiting for her response, he opened the rear door. If she didn't know better, she'd actually think he was nervous about being alone with her, but that was crazy. She couldn't imagine anything making Colton Black nervous. Following him outside, she found they were on the wide, wraparound porch. Beside the door was a swinging bench that overlooked the vastness of the surrounding countryside. Even by the dim light of the half-moon, Maddie could make out the gentle rise of hills that culminated in the distant mountains. The temperatures had dipped, and she found herself shivering a little in the night air.

"Come sit down," Colton urged and tugged her down onto the swing beside him, giving a gentle push with his foot.

Maddie held herself away from him, but she could feel his heat even across the short distance that separated them. It was all she could do not to slide closer and absorb his warmth.

"So what happens tomorrow?" she finally asked.

"Tomorrow, we get your brother back," he replied in a clipped tone.

Maddie turned to stare at him. His profile was stark, and she could see by the set of his jaw that he wouldn't welcome an argument from her.

"Why are you doing this?" she finally asked.

"Because nobody should be allowed to get away with kidnapping and extortion." He bit out the words. "This is why I studied criminal justice, why I joined the U.S. Marshals Service."

"So you always knew you wanted to go into law enforcement?"

"Pretty much."

"Where did you go to school?"

To her astonishment, he actually looked a little embarrassed. "I went to Stanford." Her surprise must have shown on her face, because he gave a small shrug. "It's where my father and my grandfather both went, so it was a foregone conclusion that I would also go."

"You said your father lives in Monterey, so I'm guessing he's not Shoshone?"

Colton laughed, and Maddie watched as it transformed his face from handsome to breathtaking. She realized she'd never seen him laugh until now, and she liked the way it sounded—deep and rich.

"No," he finally said, "my father is definitely not Shoshone." He paused. "He's a surgeon, and when he was in medical school, he spent a summer on a Shoshone reservation, working at the local medical center. That's where he met my mother."

"Oh." Maddie digested this. "So they fell in love."

Colton smiled. "For that one summer, they did. After he returned to Stanford, my mother discovered she was pregnant with me. My father offered to marry her, but she refused."

Maddie shouldn't have felt shocked, but somehow the knowledge dismayed her. She didn't know what kind of childhood she'd expected him to have, but knowing he'd come from a single-parent family made her feel sympathetic to him.

"I know what you're thinking, but you're wrong," he said, correctly reading her expression. "I had the best of both worlds, living on the reservation during the summer and in Monterey during the school year."

Maddie nodded. He was obviously close to both his parents, and she couldn't help but envy him that.

"What about you?" he asked, still rocking the swing gently. "How did you end up becoming an accountant?"

She looked at him, startled, before remembering that of course he knew she was an accountant—he knew everything about her background. Smoothing her fingers over her jeans, she gave a self-conscious shrug.

"I lost both of my parents when I was still pretty young. After that, my brother and I lived with my grandfather in that cabin." She gave a soft huff of laughter. "And that's all we did—live with him. He was the adult, but I pretty much raised my brother. I managed our finances, and have always had a knack for numbers, so becoming an accountant seemed a natural fit."

"How did you manage to get your degree and look after your brother at the same time?"

Maddie recalled those difficult days when her grandfather had insisted she attend college in Elko. He'd somehow managed to set aside enough money to pay for her tuition, as well as her room and board, and Maddie had worked nights at a local restaurant to earn extra money. But that had changed the night Jamie had turned up unexpectedly at her dorm room, saying he couldn't live in the cabin anymore.

"After I left for college, my grandfather began drinking again. Nothing Jamie did or said could change his behavior." She couldn't keep the bitterness out of her voice at the memory. "He didn't do any food shopping, or even care if Jamie went to school or not. He completely neglected his own grandson."

"So you took him in."

Maddie gave him a helpless look. "What else could I do? Jamie showed up at my dorm room at ten o'clock at night, having hitched all the way from the cabin. He was only a child!" She recalled again how horrified she had been upon discovering her twelve-year-old brother had hitchhiked along Interstate 80, alone and at night.

"So what did you do?"

"What I had to do. I left the dorm and found an apartment with two other students, and brought Jamie to live with me. He went to the local public school, and I worked nights at a nearby restaurant in order to keep up with the rent." She shrugged. "Once I graduated, I got a job and we found our own place."

"You were little more than a kid yourself."

Maddie snorted. "Trust me, I grew up fast. My mother died when Jamie was just a toddler, and my father committed suicide about a year later. Not exactly an idyllic childhood."

Colton blew out a hard breath and stared upward at the stars for a long moment. "I ran into a friend of yours the night you took my truck. An old coot named Zeke. He said to tell you hello."

"Oh, my God," Maddie groaned. "Is he still alive?"

"He is, and he certainly remembered you. Said you were a liar and a thief."

"He was right." She gave a rueful laugh. "Back then, I'd have done just about anything for a little money. God knows my grandpa wasn't doing anything to keep us solvent."

"And yet he had money to send you to college," Colton mused.

"That's what's so confusing," Maddie admitted. "We lived with next to nothing, but he had no trouble coming up with tuition money for me. I asked him so many times where he got it, but he'd just clam up. I finally decided I didn't want to know. Later on, though, when he was really sick, he'd say—" She broke off abruptly. She hadn't meant to share so much with this man. "Never mind."

"What did he say?" Reaching across the space between them, Colton laced his fingers with hers. "Tell me."

Maddie used her free hand to pinch the bridge of her nose hard, not wanting to remember those days when her grandfather had been terminally ill, and so strung out on his pain meds that she was never sure if he was lucid. But as he had from the beginning, Colton made her want to confide in him, to tell him everything.

"Toward the end, when he was in the hospital and all they could do was keep his morphine pump going, he'd say that he had a fortune hidden in the cabin." Maddie turned to look at Colton. "He said he was sitting on a gold mine."

Colton's fingers squeezed hers. "That's why you went there. You thought he had a hoard of cash stashed under the floorboards."

"Yeah." She gave a bitter laugh. "I was so stupid."

"Hey, come here." Releasing her hand, Colton slid his arm around her shoulders and pulled her across the narrow space that separated them, hugging her against his side. "There's nothing stupid about having hope."

His voice was low and a little rough, rubbing across her senses like velvet, and Maddie found she wanted to wrap him around her. He smelled good, like soap and something more elemental, something outdoorsy and masculine. She leaned into him, enjoying how solid he felt.

"Do you really think there's any hope?" she murmured. "I know what kind of guys these are, and what they're capable of." She glanced at him. "My father committed suicide because he'd lost everything at the casinos. If that wasn't bad enough, he'd borrowed the money he'd lost and had no way to repay it. He thought ending his life was preferable to what the moneylenders might do to him."

Colton's arm tightened around her shoulders. "I'm sorry you had to go through that. But I promise you that nothing is going to happen to Jamie."

Maddie nodded mutely, not trusting herself to speak. She rarely talked about her father and had never told anyone how he had died. She remembered him as a man of extreme moods; when things were going well, he'd be exuberant and generous, promising Maddie and her brother the world. But when things hadn't gone well, he'd been angry and despondent, and Maddie had taken care to keep herself and her brother out of his way. Now she swallowed hard against the emotion that those memories dredged up, and took several deep breaths.

"I believe you," she replied when she could finally speak. Surrounded by Colton's warmth and supported by his strength, Maddie realized she *did* believe him. The guy oozed confidence and capability, and he had years of experience in dealing with men like the ones who had taken Jamie. Emboldened, she reached out and placed a hand on his hard thigh. "More than that, I trust you."

His expression changed and softened, and then he was hauling her across his lap. "Ah, Maddie, you've no idea how much that means to me. Last night, I wanted to stay in that bed with you."

Sprawled across his hard thighs, with his arms clamped around her, Maddie could only stare at him in bemusement. "Then why didn't you?"

In the dim light that spilled onto the porch through the bedroom window, Maddie could just make out his expression, and something knotted low in her abdomen. Something needy.

"Because I didn't want to give you a reason to run again."

"I don't understand."

Colton's arms tightened around her. "I wanted you to trust me, Madeleine. I didn't want you to have sex with me out of some twisted sense of obligation or because you thought it was the only way I'd agree to help you." He paused. "And I didn't want to let my own guard down enough to trust you. There was a part of me that wondered if you'd wait until I fell asleep and then bolt."

She recalled how he had shackled her to the headboard while he had taken a shower, and knew that, given the chance, she probably would have left. But between last night and right now, something had changed. While she acknowledged that Colton was her best chance for getting Jamie back safely, she realized that even if he wasn't, she had no desire to leave him. She wanted to be with him, and her reasons had nothing to do with Jamie and everything to do with the raw, undeniable attraction she'd felt toward him since they'd first met.

"And now?" she ventured, daring to lay her hand against his chest, and feeling the heavy thump of his heart beneath her palm. "Would you still leave me?"

"Ah, Madeleine," he groaned, and slid one hand beneath her jaw, tipping her face up. "I don't care why you want me to stay, just as long as you let me. For tonight, let me love you."

Maddie wasn't sure who moved first, but in the next instant her arms were around his neck and he was kissing her the way she'd imagined him doing, deeply and sensuously, sending heat shimmering through her. She told herself that after tomorrow, everything might change. After she had Jamie safely back, she and Colton might very well go their separate ways and never see each other again. But for tonight, at least, this was enough.

11

AT THE FIRST touch of her tongue against his, Colton groaned and dragged her against him. She shifted on his lap, trying to get closer, and the sensation of her soft bottom against his stiff arousal was sweet torture. He wanted—he *needed*—to be inside her.

He surged to his feet, lifting Madeleine in his arms. She gasped and clutched him around the shoulders as he strode back into the bedroom, kicking the door shut behind him. He set her on her feet beside the bed, and she raised herself on tiptoes to press another kiss against his mouth.

"I think I've wanted this since the night at the cabin," she confessed with a shy smile. "When we were on the couch, and you were so sweet to me... But then you sent me to bed alone. I was actually disappointed."

Reaching behind her, Colton drew her hair free of the ponytail and threaded his fingers through the thick, silken strands, admiring how the lamplight picked out the gold highlights.

"I didn't want to take advantage of you," he said gruffly.

For a moment, guilt colored her cheeks. "I almost took advantage of you later, after I'd handcuffed you to the sofa. You looked so—so *delicious*."

"I remember," Colton said darkly, recalling how he had initially misinterpreted her intent.

Madeleine smiled and leaned up to plant another soft kiss against his mouth, drawing her tongue along the seam of his lips until he groaned in defeat and dragged her closer, sliding his hands over her back to cup her rear and pull her against his hips.

"I'll make it up to you," she whispered against his mouth.

Her hands went to his belt, and Colton leaned back just enough to allow her to work the buckle. She caught her lower lip between her teeth as she concentrated, until he put his hands over hers.

"I've got this," he said, his voice little more than a growl.

He wasn't sure he'd be able to control himself if she actually put her hands on him. He'd been aroused since she'd told him she wanted him to stay, but he didn't want to rush this. He wanted to make it good for Madeleine, for both of them.

Bracketing her face in his hands, he lowered his mouth to hers, covering her lips with his own. She made a sound of approval and shifted closer, her palms resting lightly at his waist. But when he angled his head for a better fit, deepening the kiss, she pressed against him, sliding her hands around to his back. She pushed past his teeth, sweeping her tongue against his and ramping up his need.

Slowly, he walked her backward until her knees hit the bed, and then he lowered her onto the mattress, following her body with the length of his own. He didn't break the kiss, but continued to feast on her mouth as he pulled her T-shirt free from the waistband of her jeans and stroked his hand over her stomach. Her skin was smooth and warm, and he slid his palm upward until he encountered the rise of one breast.

Madeleine dragged her mouth away from his and reached down to cover his hand with her own. Beneath the lacy bra, he could feel her nipple thrusting against his palm.

"Touch me," she whispered.

Colton stared at her face. Her skin was flushed, her pupils so dilated that they almost swallowed up the surrounding irises. Her mouth was swollen and pink from his kisses, and her breath came in soft pants.

"Darlin'," he rasped, "I want to touch you so badly, but I need to take it slow."

"Then go slow, but please—touch me."

Colton needed no further encouragement. Rearing back, he caught the hem of her shirt and dragged it upward. Madeleine helped him by sitting up and pulling it over her head and then tossing it onto the floor. Reaching behind her back, she quickly unfastened the bra and let the straps slide down her arms, until the insubstantial garment fell into her lap.

Colton's breath caught. Though he'd seen her before, he was left incoherent now. Her skin was creamy and pale, her breasts full and pink-tipped. With her honey-colored hair spilling over her shoulders, she looked like every fantasy he'd ever had. He wanted to lick her all over.

"You're beautiful," he finally managed to say, and he meant it. He'd never seen a woman as elegantly feminine as Madeleine Howe, and without conscious thought, he reached out and covered one breast with his hand. She drew in a sharp breath and arched into his palm, and then covered his hand with her own, pressing his fingers against her flesh.

"This is what I want," she said with feeling, her gaze clinging to his. "Please, Colton…"

"Ah, Madeleine," he replied, helpless to resist her. With his hand still covering her, he eased her back onto the bed. "Tell me what you want, what you like."

"This," she assured him, and drew him down for a kiss.

The slide of her tongue against his was sweet and hot, and beneath his fingertips, her nipple tightened even more. Lust jackknifed through him, and with a groan, Colton pressed deeper, sweeping his tongue past her teeth to explore her more fully. She moaned softly and surged upward against him. Dragging his mouth from hers, Colton scattered fevered kisses along the length of her throat, over the fragile line of her collarbones until he reached the soft swell of her breast.

He cupped her in his hand and stroked his thumb over the distended tip, watching as the pink nub tightened beneath his touch. Madeleine gasped softly, and when Colton bent his head to capture her nipple in his mouth, she tunneled her fingers into his hair, holding him there. She was soft and supple, and the small sounds of pleasure she made as he suckled her caused his body to tighten in response.

He worked his way down her torso, kissing the undersides of her breasts and her firm, flat stomach before his fingers went to the button of her jeans. He glanced up at her, taking in her flushed face and tumbled hair, and letting his gaze linger on her breasts, which rose and fell with her rapid breathing.

"Do you need some help?" she asked, her eyes twinkling.

In answer, Colton unfastened her pants and dragged the zipper down before skating his tongue over the satiny skin he'd exposed. The lacy edge of her pale yellow panties lured him on, and hooking his fingers into the waistband of her jeans, he tugged them down over her hips. Through the nearly sheer fabric of her panties, he could see a dark triangle of curls.

"Finally," he muttered, and bent his head to press his mouth against the material.

"Finally—what?"

Colton lifted his head long enough to meet Madeleine's eyes. "Finally, I get to see you—all of you," he replied. "Last night was amazing, but too damned dark for me."

"And I was just about to suggest we dim the lights."

"Over my dead body," he growled. Reaching down, he tugged her sneakers from her feet. "Now take these pants off."

Madeleine giggled at his impatience, and he threw

her a surprised glance. She looked rosy and tousled, and so incredibly sexy that he wanted to toss his good intentions out the window and take her hard and fast. He realized he'd never heard her giggle, and he liked the sound of it.

He would have liked to look at her as she lay there in nothing but her yellow panties, but she reached down and dragged him upward, curling one leg over his to keep him from retreating.

"Now it's my turn," she murmured, and slid her hands beneath the hem of his T-shirt, pushing it up over his chest. Colton helped her by reaching behind his head and grabbing a fistful of the material to drag the shirt off and fling it onto the floor beside her pants.

He was gratified when Madeleine's eyes widened, and she reached up to stroke her hands over his shoulders and down his chest, her fingers lingering on his pecs. "You're so gorgeous."

He gave a huff of embarrassed laughter. "Those are supposed to be my words."

Bracing his hands on either side of her, he bent his head and caught her mouth with his, feasting on her lips and welcoming the soft thrust of her tongue against his. She arched upward, sliding her arms around him and stroking the length of his spine with her fingers. This time, when her hands moved to the front of his pants and unfastened them, he made no move to stop her. She dragged the zipper down and then hooked her fingers in both his jeans and boxers, pushing them down. Colton helped her, kicking his boots off and removing the rest of his clothes.

Madeleine's gaze drifted over him, lingering on his stiff erection. He came back over her, and she reached between their bodies and curled her fingers around the straining length. When she slid her hand experimentally along his shaft, Colton groaned loudly and bent his forehead to hers, struggling to maintain some control.

"You're so hard," she breathed and squeezed him gently. "And so hot."

After using his leg to nudge her thighs apart, Colton settled between them, keeping his weight on his elbows. But when Madeleine guided the head of his penis to her slick center, he reared back.

"Darlin', wait." Disentangling himself from her, he rose and quickly searched through the backpack until he retrieved a box of condoms. He tore the box open as he returned to the bed, placing several foil packets within easy reach on the bedside table.

"I picked these up while I was out today," he said, lowering himself beside her.

Madeleine smiled. "You're very confident in yourself."

"No, darlin'," he rasped, bending to tease one breast with his tongue. "Just hopeful."

She drew in a sharp breath at the sensation. When he slid one hand down the length of her body and played with the soft curls at the juncture of her thighs, her legs fell open, inviting him to explore farther. Colton needed no further invitation. He stroked his fingers over her through the fragile barrier of her panties, noting with satisfaction that she was already damp. She shifted restlessly beneath him, her hands smoothing over his back and shoulders as he kissed his way down the length of her body.

"I want to taste you again," he growled when he reached the lacy edge of her panties.

"Colton—"

"Shh."

Repositioning himself at the foot of the bed, he slowly drew her underwear down, drinking in the sight of her slender hips and pale skin. She didn't protest again, but when he discarded the scrap of lingerie, she pressed her knees together, shielding herself from his view.

"Madeleine," he said softly, "open your legs. Let me see you."

She pressed her hands over her face. "But it's so bright in here!"

"Okay," he said, smiling at her uncharacteristic shyness. Rising, he strode to the door and flipped off the lights, locking the door at the same time. Then he turned on the bathroom light, leaving the door open just enough to softly illuminate the bedroom.

Climbing over her, he tugged her hands away from her face and kissed her, until he felt her body begin to relax and respond, and her arms came around him once more. When she began to arch against him again, he smoothed his hand down her stomach and then lower. This time, she opened readily for him, and he cupped her in his palm, feeling her heat and incredible softness.

"You feel so good," he whispered, skating his lips over her jaw. "Like the finest satin."

Reaching down, she curled her hand around him and

stroked him, tentatively at first, and then more firmly. "You feel like hot steel," she breathed against his mouth. "I want you inside me."

Her words, combined with the erotic slide of her fingers over his aroused flesh, caused heat to gather in his groin, and he felt himself swell in her hand.

"Soon," he promised, and parted her damp flesh with his fingers, using one fingertip to swirl her moisture around and over the small rise of her clitoris. She drew in a hiss, and as if mimicking his movements, ran her thumb over the head of his erection, where he knew she would find a drop of fluid.

He continued to touch her, rubbing his fingers over her, until she released him and clutched at the bed-clothes instead, beginning to writhe. Sliding to the foot of the bed, Colton continued his rhythmic movements, but now he bent his head and touched his tongue to her, licking along the seam of her sex. She made a whimpering sound of need and pushed her hips toward him.

"Oh, sweetheart," he groaned, "you are so damned gorgeous down here."

Using his fingers to part her, Colton swept his tongue over her, concentrating on the aroused nub of flesh, even as he eased a finger into her and began thrusting gently. She was hot and tight and so aroused that he thought he might lose control just from giving her pleasure and listening to the noises she made.

Glancing up the length of her body, he saw she was on her elbows, watching him through eyes that were slightly unfocused. Her breasts heaved with her rising excitement, and she pushed weakly at him with one hand.

"No more," she begged, "or I won't last."

Reluctantly, Colton released her and pulled himself up to lie beside her, drawing her against him. She wound her arms around his neck, pushing her fingers into his hair and holding his head in place as she speared her tongue against his.

"That felt incredible, and I was so close," she said against his lips. "But this time, I want to see you come with me."

Colton groaned and, reaching beyond her, snagged a condom from the bedside table. But when he would have torn it open with his teeth and rolled it on, she gripped his hand, stopping him. He gave her a look of barely contained impatience.

"Madeleine, don't," he said, his voice rough with need. "If I'm not inside you in the next five seconds, I'm going to be the one who won't last."

To his astonishment, she pushed against his shoulders until he was forced to lie back against the pillows.

"You will be inside me," she said in a husky voice. "Just not the way you think."

She pressed a soft, moist kiss against his mouth and then began to work her way down his body, alternately licking and biting the length of his chest and stomach, even as her hand curled around his straining erection. Colton knew where she was going, and his balls tightened in anticipation. Still, he had to be sure.

"Maddie," he rasped, "you don't have to do this."

She lifted her head and looked at him, and then

smiled a wide, beatific smile. "I know I don't have to. I *want* to do this."

As Colton watched in astonished delight, she dipped her head and delicately ran her tongue along the length of him. He shuddered at the sensation, and when she took him in her mouth and drew on him, he dropped his head back and groaned loudly.

"Do you like that?"

Colton glanced up to find her watching him, even as she continued to stroke him with her hand.

"Oh, yeah," he said, his voice low and rough. Reaching out, he tucked a strand of hair behind her ear and drew the back of his knuckles lightly along her jaw. "That feels incredible."

Keeping her eyes on him, she wrapped her lips around him once more, and Colton had to grit his teeth to keep from losing it big time. Watching her was a huge turn-on, but he needed to slow things down. He let her stroke him with her mouth and tongue for another minute until his balls begin to tighten.

"Come here," he commanded, and pulled her up until she lay sprawled on top of him, her hair falling around their faces in a fragrant curtain. "If I don't stop you, this whole thing is going to be over real quick."

Madeleine smiled and stroked her thumb over his lower lip, fixing her attention on his mouth. "Well, we don't want that." Dipping her head, she gave him a heated kiss and slowly rubbed herself over his aching flesh. Colton groaned into her mouth, and in one fluid movement, flipped her onto her back so that she lay beneath him. Her eyes widened as she realized he was right *there*.

"Colton…" She arched upward, rubbing sensuously against him. "I want you inside of me."

Colton tore the condom open, rearing back on his knees just long enough to cover himself. She reached for him and guided him to her center, positioning him at her entrance. But Colton held back, resisting the urge to immediately sink into her welcoming body.

"Are you sure about this?"

She urged him closer. "God, yes." Her eyes were slumberous with desire. "I've wanted you since that night at the cabin, when I handcuffed you to the sofa."

Colton felt a smile tilt his lips. "So bondage excites you? I'll remember that."

Madeleine raised her knees, pressing her heels against the back of his thighs. "That only works when I have *you* restrained," she said breathlessly. "Please, Colton…"

In answer, he pushed her hands over her head and held them there before bending to nuzzle one breast, flicking her nipple with his tongue before drawing the sensitized flesh into his mouth. Madeleine squirmed beneath him and tried to free her hands to no avail. He held her firmly in place as he worked his way upward, skating his lips over her throat and neck and sensing her mounting excitement.

"So bondage doesn't turn you on?" He caught her earlobe between his teeth.

"No. You do," she panted. "Please…"

Her soft plea, combined with the warm slide of her body against his, was too much. Nudging her thighs farther apart, he began to ease himself into her heat, gritting his teeth against the exquisite sensation. She was tight and hot, and her inner muscles gripped him like a sleek, silken fist. Releasing her hands, he braced his weight on his elbows and kissed her hard, mating his tongue with hers even as he pushed himself deeper.

Madeleine gripped his buttocks, urging him on. "Don't hold back," she breathed against his mouth. "I want all of you."

Lust flooded through him, a savage need to claim her, and he drove into her, harder and faster. She made a whimpering sound of need, and drew her knees up to hook her ankles around the small of his back, rising to meet each thrust with an urgency that matched his own raw hunger. He was so close, but he could see from Madeleine's expression that she strained for release. Shifting slightly, he adjusted the angle of his movements to provide her with the friction she needed. Almost immediately, she gave a soft cry, and he felt her tighten around him. A shudder rippled through her, and she arched upward, her mouth open on a soundless cry of pleasure. Her face as she reached orgasm was so sexy that Colton felt heat building at the base of his spine, and the sensation of her body fisting tightly around him was too much. He gave a hoarse shout as he came in a white-hot rush of ecstasy.

For several long moments, he was incapable of moving. The only sound in the room was their uneven breathing. Madeleine's hands roamed over his back, languidly stroking his skin. As Colton slowly came back to earth, he realized he was crushing her into the mattress. With a groan, he rolled to the side, pulling her with him. He pressed his lips against her hair, breathing in her fragrance.

"Are you okay?"

She nodded and curled closer, sliding one hand over his ribs. "Oh, yeah. That was…amazing."

Her voice sounded drowsy and content. Colton had to agree with her; he couldn't recall the last time he'd had such mind-blowing sex. But there was a part of him that was also terrified. If he'd thought he was in over his head this morning, now he was convinced of it.

He'd promised himself that he wouldn't sleep with her until she'd shared all her secrets with him. And she had. But now he was the one with secrets, and he couldn't help but wonder how she would feel once she discovered them.

Reaching down, Colton dragged the covers over them both, and hugged her closer. Rolling against him, Madeleine pressed a kiss against his chest, directly over his heart.

"Don't let me fall asleep," she murmured.

He felt his mouth twitch with a smile. "Why not?"

She yawned hugely and curled herself around him. "Because I don't trust you not to leave me."

Something tightened in Colton's chest. Tipping her face up, he kissed her softly. "Go to sleep," he said against her lips. "When I wake you up in a few hours, I promise it won't be because I'm leaving."

BUT WHEN MADDIE woke up, she was alone. She didn't need to look to know there was nobody beside her in the big bed. The room was still shrouded in shadows, but she could see the first fingers of light beginning to creep through the windows. What time was it? She turned on her side to peer at the bedside clock, only to find both her hands restrained over her head. In dismay, she twisted to discover her wrists manacled to the headboard with Colton's handcuffs.

Struggling to an upright position, she yanked fruitlessly at the restraints. The blankets fell away, and she realized that not only had Colton shackled her to the bed, he'd left her naked and feeling helpless at being exposed this way to whoever might come to her rescue.

Worse, he'd left her behind while he carried out whatever plan he and his buddies had devised to rescue her brother. Maddie couldn't believe he'd done this to her, even after last night.

Especially after last night.

He'd promised that he wouldn't leave, and yet he'd slipped away like a thief in the night while she slept. Furious over his betrayal, Maddie wanted to scream in frustration, even as she wanted to weep with disappointment.

She had trusted him.

She sagged against the pillows, telling herself she wouldn't cry. She had no idea how she was going to explain her present predicament to Colton's mother, but she'd figure it out. God knew she'd been in worse situations. And when she finally did get free—

"Well, this sure is a pretty sight," drawled a masculine voice from the doorway.

Maddie snapped her head around to see Colton lounging in the open door of the bedroom, a steaming mug of coffee in one hand. Relief surged through her, so raw and strong that for a moment all the strength drained from her body, and she could only stare helplessly at him.

He hadn't left.

He wore nothing but a pair of faded blue jeans, and the sight of his sleek, sculpted muscles made Maddie's mouth go dry. He looked incredibly sexy, and as his dark eyes traveled leisurely over her body, she became aware of the fact that she was completely nude.

And handcuffed to the bed.

"Colton." She rattled the metal cuffs. "Release me right now. I can't believe you left me here like this!"

He stepped into the room, kicking the bedroom door closed behind him with one bare foot. A wicked dimple flashed in one lean cheek as he approached the bed and placed the mug of coffee on the bedside table. Ignoring her outrage, he sat down on the edge of the mattress and studied her with frank appreciation.

"So now you know what it feels like to wake up and find yourself handcuffed to a piece of furniture and unable to do anything about it," he murmured thoughtfully.

"I said I was sorry." She yanked again at the cuffs.

"Let me loose. What time is it, anyway? We should get going."

"It's barely 5:00 a.m., and you are not going anywhere," Colton said firmly. Reaching out, he caught a tendril of her hair and wound it lazily around his finger. "You need to trust me, Madeleine."

She watched him warily. "I do."

He tugged on her hair, drawing her face closer to his. "I'm not so sure."

Maddie searched his face, trying to assess his mood, but his nearness caused her pulse to kick up a notch, and all she could think was how absolutely gorgeous he looked first thing in the morning.

"I already told you that I trust you." She tried to sound annoyed, but her voice came out a little breathless.

"Then do what I tell you to do," he said softly, and his gaze dropped downward, searing her skin wherever it touched

"Colton…"

She didn't like this game. Didn't like the surge of anticipation that leaped through her veins, or the immediate gathering of heat at her core as she wondered what he might have in mind.

Tugging her face closer, he searched her eyes, his lips a fraction from her own. "Lie back on the pillows, Madeleine."

Before he had finished uttering her name, his mouth was on hers, working softly and sensuously as he pressed her down. While he kissed her, his hands roamed freely over her body, caressing her breasts and skimming over her waist and hips. With her arms secured over her head, Maddie could only shift restlessly beneath him, when what she really wanted was to touch him everywhere.

"Unfasten me," she breathed against his mouth.

She felt him smile against her skin, and then he began working his way down the length of her body, licking and nibbling. Maddie watched him, her body already primed for what she knew was coming. When he eased one hand between her thighs and slid a finger through her folds, she had to swallow a moan of pleasure.

"Don't hold back," he said, scraping his teeth along the rise of her hip bone. "Isn't that what you said to me?"

Her breathing was shallow now, and when he slid two fingers inside her, she was helpless to prevent herself from pushing against his hand. Colton chuckled softly. "I thought you said bondage didn't turn you on," he said in a wicked whisper. "I'm glad you were wrong."

Then he dipped his head and licked her, using his fingers and tongue to drive her wild. Maddie stopped struggling and gave herself over to the pleasure, acknowledging that this was what she wanted. This man, focusing all his masculine attention on her, making her feel beautiful and sexy, and so aroused that she knew she wouldn't last very long.

Colton pulled back enough to study her in the indistinct light, before swirling his tongue over her clitoris. Heat shimmered through her, and her heartbeat throbbed in every limb. Desire tightened her inner muscles, gathered at her core and spiraled upward, pulling her with it, until suddenly it exploded in a brilliant release of sparks.

Maddie heard herself cry out as wave after wave of pleasure crashed over her, but Colton didn't stop until he'd wrung every last shudder from her trembling body. Only when she lay panting and replete, unable to muster up the slightest resistance, did he finally pull himself up to lie beside her. Reaching beneath his pillow, he withdrew a small key, fitted it into the handcuffs and released her. Then he gathered her into his arms until her face was pressed against his shoulder.

"Tell me." His voice was an insistent rumble against her ear.

Maddie didn't have to ask what he wanted; she knew. She closed her eyes and swallowed hard. "I trust you."

"Then you won't argue with me when I tell you that you can't come with me to Reno."

Maddie snapped her head up to meet Colton's eyes. His gaze was steady, his expression implacable. She knew he wasn't completely unaffected by what had just happened between them. His arousal was evident beneath his jeans, and his pulse beat strongly at the base of his throat. But there was something steely in his manner that told Maddie no amount of begging or pleading would change his mind.

Slowly, she withdrew from his arms and put some space between them, dragging the sheet over her nudity. Her body still thrummed from his touch, but inside she was slowly growing cold. Sitting up, she clutched the fabric beneath her chin and swung her legs to the floor.

"No problem." She forced herself to stand up and

face him. He looked like a fantasy come true, lying on the bed wearing only his jeans, his body layered in sleek, bronzed muscle. She had to fight the constriction in her throat. "I can do this without you. I don't need you."

_12_

SOMETHING TIGHTENED PAINFULLY in Colton's chest at her words. Even knowing she didn't mean what she said, he couldn't prevent the sharp stab of regret that sliced through him.

She still didn't trust him.

He sat up on the edge of the bed, trying not to let her see how deeply her words impacted him. "Madeleine, try to understand. There's too much risk involved. You don't know what these men are capable of. They're career criminals with a network that extends across the country. They're suspected of committing at least four murders. I won't risk you getting hurt or killed."

Wrapping the sheet tighter around her body, Madeleine glared at him. Colton wondered if she had any clue just how magnificent she looked, with her hair tumbling around her shoulders and her eyes shooting gold sparks.

"If that's true, then there's no way I'm staying here," she said fiercely. "You are not leaving me behind. He's my brother, and nothing will prevent me from being in Reno at ten o'clock."

Colton stood up and took a step toward her. She clutched the sheet a little tighter, but didn't retreat, even when he invaded her personal space. She tipped her chin up instead, defiant.

"And then what?" he demanded. "How are you going to pay them?"

He thought he saw a flare of distress in her hazel eyes, but she turned away and began snatching her clothing from the floor, dressing in jerky movements while trying to keep the sheet firmly in place. Frustrated, Colton scrubbed a hand over his head.

"Just get dressed," he finally said. "It's not like I haven't already seen everything."

"Yes, that was quite the performance," she muttered, yanking her jeans on over her hips and shoving her arms through the sleeves of her shirt. "Sleep with me and get me to trust you when all the while you intended to ditch me." She gave a bitter laugh. "When I think I could have been at the casinos, raking in the money I need to save Jamie. Instead, I've just been wasting my time."

Anger surged through Colton at the insinuation that their lovemaking had meant so little to her. She pulled her sneakers on, her body rigid. Colton grasped her arm and turned her toward him.

"Is that what last night was to you? A waste of time?"

She tipped her chin up and jerked free of his grasp. "Why don't we just call it what it was—your pound of flesh?"

He recoiled, stunned. "That's bullshit and you know it."

"Is it?"

She held his gaze, but Colton saw the real fear in her eyes. In a flash, he realized her words were nothing but a shield to hide her true feelings, and his anger evaporated. She was terrified, not only for her brother's safety, but by the suspicion that he might have used her.

"Madeleine," he said, softening his tone. "You'd never have won enough money at the casinos to pay his debt. Those security guards were onto you after you'd won a couple grand. Do you think they wouldn't have noticed if you'd started to win even more? By now the casinos will have red-flagged you. The likelihood of you getting near another blackjack table is about zero."

"Maybe so," she conceded, "but I can't just sit around doing nothing." Her expression was almost desperate. "Please, Colton, I'll go crazy if you leave me behind. He's my brother. You have to take me with you. Those men will expect me to be there!"

Colton wanted badly to haul her into his arms, but he could see she wouldn't welcome that. She was edgy and emotional, and on the very brink of ditching him completely and taking matters into her own hands. He knew Aiden and Siyota were already in position, but the thought of Madeleine being anywhere near the abandoned mine filled him with fear. Drawing in a deep breath, he decided the only way to convince her to stay behind was to tell her the truth.

"Madeleine, listen to me," he said carefully. He caught her upper arms, drawing her toward him. She watched him warily, but didn't pull away.

"Last night was amazing," he said, letting her see the truth in his eyes. "You and I haven't known each other for all that long, but I'm beginning to think that you taking me hostage was meant to be."

A frown puckered her forehead. "What do you mean?"

"I mean that of all the people you could have ended up with, you're with someone who knows exactly the kind of men we're dealing with." He paused and dipped his head to look directly into her eyes. "Which is why I don't want you anywhere near them."

"Colton—" She stiffened in his arms and began to pull back.

"Madeleine, sweetheart." He put a finger beneath her chin and raised her face, forcing her to look at him. "I think I'm falling in love with you, but if I let you go to that mine and something happens to you, we'll never have the chance to find out what it is we might have had together."

He watched as her eyes widened and her mouth parted on a soft "oh" of surprise. But everything he'd said was true. He was falling for her in a big way, and the thought of deliberately placing her in danger went against every instinct he had.

He thought he could see a sheen of tears in her eyes. "Colton," she finally said, "there are things you don't know about me, things I've done...."

Colton hauled her into his arms, feeling her resistance melt. "I know all I need to know, like the fact that you're willing to risk everything for those you love. I know you did things when you were younger that you're not proud of, but I know you did them to keep what was left of your family together." He leaned back enough to look at her face. "I think you take insane risks, but I get why you do it."

Now there was no mistaking her tears. "Colton, I don't know what to say. But if these men are as bad as you think they are, what makes you think I want you risking *your* life?"

He gave her a lopsided grin. "Is that your way of saying you might care for me a little?"

Madeleine gave a choked laugh and raised herself on her toes to press a lingering kiss against his mouth. "Let me show you how much I care for you," she whispered against his lips. "How much time do I have?"

Colton's heart skipped a beat. "We need to be on the road within the hour."

"Perfect," she breathed. She wound her arms around his neck and led him, unresisting, toward the bed.

MADDIE SAT IN the passenger seat of the truck and waved through the window at Colton's mother as they pulled away from the ranch. Maddie still felt a little overwhelmed by the events of the past day, and how his family had welcomed her so completely. But more than that, she couldn't stop thinking about how Colton had made love to her that morning. If she'd had any doubts about his feelings for her, they'd been completely dispelled by the intensity of his lovemaking. He'd been both tender and fierce and had held for a long time afterward. When he'd finally told her she could go with him to the mine, she'd been weak with relief.

She still couldn't quite comprehend that this magnificent man could be falling for her. Until now, her own feelings toward him had been a confusing mixture of desire, attraction and frustration. Only when she realized he'd be putting his own life on the line for her brother did she understand the extent of her growing feelings for him. Just the thought of something happening to Colton terrified her. They'd known each other only a few days, yet he was quickly becoming the center of her world. She'd never had anyone make her feel as safe and as precious as he did, and she was racked with guilt that her first thought was for his safety and not Jamie's.

"I'm letting you come with me on the condition that you do exactly as I tell you," Colton was saying now. He glanced away from the road long enough to send her a meaningful look. "Understood?"

Maddie nodded. "Yes. I'll do whatever you tell me to."

She meant it. She was so grateful that he had changed his mind and agreed to bring her with him that she would have readily agreed to any of the conditions he imposed.

"I don't like that these bastards will even get a look at you," he grumbled.

Maddie had argued that the moneylenders would expect her to bring the cash, and if she wasn't there, they might actually kill Jamie. In the end, Colton had relented, but only reluctantly.

"Your law enforcement friends will be there," she countered. "You said yourself that they had a good plan."

"I've learned from experience to expect the unexpected," he muttered.

Maddie didn't want to think about all the things that could go wrong. She just wanted to get to the happy ending, where she had both Jamie and Colton out of harm's way. She could see how tense Colton was, and knew he was still trying to figure out how to make the exchange without involving her. She searched around in her mind for a way to distract him.

"What did your mother call me when we were saying goodbye?" she asked. "She said it was my Shoshone name."

Colton's mouth tilted in a half smile. "She called you Tadita." He glanced at her, one sweeping look that took in everything, and made Maddie feel as if he had just seen into her soul. "It means One Who Runs."

"Oh." Maddie digested this in silence. "What's your Shoshone name?"

"Kajika. It means Walks without Sound."

She gave a small laugh. "Wow. That's pretty accurate."

"For you or for me?"

Maddie turned to look at him. "For both of us. I feel as if I've been running since I was a kid."

Colton reached across the console and covered her hand with his, startling her. "Don't you think it's time you stopped?"

"I'm trying. I've told myself so often that I'm a respectable member of society, I've almost fallen for my own con."

He gave her a quizzical look and squeezed her hand.

"What are you talking about? I've seen the worst side of human nature and society, and, darlin', I can tell you with absolute certainty that you are more than respectable."

Maddie appreciated his words, but when she considered her upbringing, and even the current trouble that Jamie had gotten himself into, she wasn't so sure she believed him. She'd worked hard to get where she was, but sometimes she felt her life was a sham. Eventually, someone was going to figure it out, and then she'd lose everything.

Again.

"What if I told you that I enjoyed winning that money at the blackjack table?" she asked quietly. "What if I said there was a part of me that missed that lifestyle?"

"I'd say you're not being completely honest. Is that really the kind of life you'd want for yourself?" he asked quietly. "Or for your brother?"

"No," she conceded. "Of course not. But sometimes I worry that what I can give him won't be enough."

"He's twenty years old, Madeleine. You've given him plenty. The best thing you can give him now—once we get him back, of course—is some solid advice and a dope slap to the back of his head."

Maddie laughed. She could picture Colton doing that with his own brothers.

They were less than five miles from the outskirts of Reno when Colton pulled off the highway and into the parking lot of an auto repair shop.

"What are we doing?" she asked.

Colton drew the truck alongside a parked car and

turned off the ignition. "We're switching vehicles," he replied, checking his watch. "Once you make the call, I'll drive you out to the mining site."

Maddie watched as he reached across her knees and opened the glove apartment to withdraw a pistol. She stared at him.

"Has that gun been there this whole time?"

Colton slanted her one grim look as he checked the cartridge, and then slid the weapon into the back of his waistband. "Yes."

"Even that night I took the truck?"

"Yes. Which was why I was so desperate to find you."

Maddie suppressed a smile. "Was that the only reason?"

He didn't look at her as he reached behind his seat, then handed her a bulletproof vest, but Maddie didn't miss the smile that curved his mouth.

"Here, put this on."

"Is this what I think it is?" She knew her voice betrayed her alarm, but she was suddenly aware of just how dangerous this could get.

"It's for your own protection. You should wear it under your clothes, so take off your T-shirt."

Maddie pulled it over her head, and made no protest as he helped her into the vest, securing the Velcro fastenings for her. Once he was satisfied, he handed her shirt back to her, helping to tug it into place.

"The T-shirt is baggy enough that you can hardly notice it," he said, surveying her critically.

"It's so heavy."

"Stop complaining," he chided her gently. "This could save your life."

"What about you? Will you be wearing one, too?"

Instead of answering her, he reached behind his seat again and retrieved his backpack, dumping it on her lap.

"You'll want to hang on to that."

"What's in here?" Maddie unzipped the top and peeked inside. What she saw made her gasp. She turned to Colton, stunned. "Where did you get this?"

He arched one black eyebrow. "What did you think we were going to use to get your brother back? Wampum?"

Maddie frowned. "I never asked you for the money."

"No, you didn't."

"So I'm guessing this is on temporary loan from the U.S. Marshals Service?"

Colton shrugged. "You can't get your brother back unless you have something to give in return."

"I don't want you to get in trouble if something goes wrong and you end up losing the cash."

To her surprise, Colton grinned. "I promise you, I am not going to lose that money." He sobered. "It's time for you to make that call."

Maddie checked the clock on the dashboard, shocked to see that it was already ten o'clock. Pulling her cell phone out, she drew in a deep breath, aware that her heart had begun to pound hard in her chest. With her eyes on Colton, she redialed the number from the previous day.

"Where are you?" snarled a male voice.

"I—I'm just outside of Reno," Maddie stuttered.

"Take Highway 80 to Exit 99. Head north five miles until you see the turnoff to the abandoned silver mine. Follow that road to the mine complex, but do not—I repeat, do not—drive into the complex. Park by the gate and walk the rest of the way. And come alone. We'll be watching."

Before Maddie could utter a word in response, the line went dead. She stared blankly at the phone for a moment, before turning to Colton. "He didn't even let me speak."

"What did they say?"

"You were right. He wants me to go to the abandoned silver mine off Highway 80. He said to park by the gate and walk in, and to go alone."

She shivered.

"Hey, come here." Reaching across the seat, Colton pulled her into his arms, hugging her tightly. "I'm going to be right there. You're not going to do anything alone, okay?"

"You can't come with me," she protested, her voice muffled against his chest. "It's too dangerous."

She felt his body vibrate with quiet laughter. Then he tipped her face up and searched her eyes, his expression one of tender exasperation. "Maddie Howe, when are you going to learn to trust me?"

She felt herself go a little weak beneath his scrutiny, and she blushed. "Maybe I need another lesson in trust building," she suggested, feeling shy.

He kissed her sweetly, bracketing her face in his big hands. "With pleasure," he said against her mouth.

"We'll start tonight. But right now we need to get going."

Maddie nodded, willing herself to remain calm. She told herself again that Colton knew what he was doing. He specialized in outsmarting the bad guys, and she just needed to trust him. She climbed out of the truck, gingerly holding the backpack of money.

Crouching down by the front of the car, Colton reached under the wheel well and withdrew a car key. Unlocking the doors, he indicated that she should drive.

"You're going to let me out about a half mile from the entrance. Then you'll park at the gate, and you'll walk twenty paces, drop the backpack and then return to the car. Understood?"

Maddie frowned. "Shouldn't I wait for them to bring Jamie out?"

"No. I want you to drop the money and get your ass back into this vehicle." Seeing her expression, his own grew hard. "I'm dead serious, Madeleine."

"Okay, fine," she said reluctantly. "Where will you be?"

"I'll be positioned where I can protect both you and your brother." His voice told her that the less she knew, the better.

"Be careful."

She knew Colton had his own misgivings about what they were about to do, especially regarding her own role in getting Jamie back. She also knew that as much as Colton wanted her to trust him, he also needed to trust her. There was no way she was going to screw this up, not when she had so much to lose.

They drove in silence until they reached the turnoff to the abandoned mine. Maddie realized her heart was racing and her breathing was shallow. She slid a glance toward Colton.

"Your brother is going to be fine," he assured her. "Just remember to drop the bag and get your ass back to the taxi. No heroics."

Maddie nodded, but her palms were moist, and she couldn't prevent her imagination from conjuring up lurid images of worst-case scenarios. Before long, they turned off the main road, and she caught a glimpse of a weather-beaten sign indicating the direction of Murray's Silver Mine. As they drove, the road gradually deteriorated, until it was little more than a gravel trail, deep with ruts, and with nothing on either side except dusty hills. Scrubby trees and sagebrush dotted the landscape, and enormous boulders and rock formations broke the unrelenting bleakness of the landscape.

"Let me out here," Colton finally directed.

Maddie slowed the car, and he turned to look at her, his hand on the door. "This will be over soon," he promised. "Everything is going to be fine."

Maddie swallowed hard and nodded.

She watched Colton step off the road, and then he vanished behind a line of craggy rocks. Drawing a deep breath, she continued along the dirt road and finally drew to a stop at a chain-link fence that blocked any farther progress. Beyond the broken gate, the road continued toward an ancient complex of buildings and outhouses. The largest, a three-story structure that looked as if it had been built a hundred years earlier, leaned precariously to one side. Beyond the buildings was the entrance to the mine itself. It consisted of a vertical shaft that opened directly into the ground, identifiable by the dilapidated hoisting house that had been erected over it. Miners would be lowered into the hole inside a cage attached to a cable. The entire mining operation looked like a ghostly remnant from the Wild West.

Maddie drew in a deep breath. The mining site had an ominous feel to it, and as she climbed out of the car, she had the eerie sensation of being watched. She hitched the backpack over one shoulder and slowly made her way through the broken gate and along the road. Her feet kicked up small clouds of dust, and the sun beat down on her head and shoulders. The protective vest was heavy, and a trickle of moisture made its way between her breasts. Maddie was acutely aware of the silence that surrounded her. She was tempted to look back over her shoulder, to see if she could spot either Colton or any of the other men, but she didn't dare.

As she drew alongside the first building, a small clapboard structure dark with age and weather, she thought she detected movement behind the dusty windows. The thought of someone watching her—someone who might want to hurt her—was almost enough to make her bolt. Instead, she continued walking, pretending she hadn't noticed the furtive activity.

She had reached the point in the road where Colton had instructed her to drop the backpack and return to the car, but her attention was riveted on the main building, where she could hear raised voices from inside.

As she cautiously took several more steps, the door

of the building opened abruptly, and her brother was thrust out. He blinked in the bright sunlight and staggered several feet toward her before collapsing to his knees in the dust.

Maddie gasped in horror.

His hands were tied behind his back, and even from a distance she could see he had been severely beaten. His face was swollen and discolored, and one eye was completely shut. Blood oozed from several cuts on his face and neck, and his shirt was filthy and torn. Blond head bowed, he knelt in the dirt, swaying as if he might pass out.

Forgetting Colton's instructions, Maddie bolted forward, only to have the ground around her feet erupt in a series of tiny dust clouds. At the same time, she became aware of the sound of rapid gunfire, and realized they were shooting at her! She skidded to a stop, unable to drag her gaze from her brother.

"Stop! Don't hurt her!" Jamie was crying, his tears mixing with the blood and dirt on his face as he tried to crawl toward her. "Please don't hurt her."

"Jamie, stay there," she urged, terrified that he would be shot and killed.

Two men emerged from the building, one of them holding what looked like a semiautomatic rifle, and the other brandishing a pistol. Both were big and burly, and Maddie guessed them to be in their late thirties. The man with the pistol turned his gun on her, while the other kept a watchful lookout, continually sweeping his rifle around the area.

"Drop the backpack," shouted the first man, and

Maddie recognized his voice, from talking with him on the phone. His expression was so cold and impassive that her first instinct was to obey him. She felt certain he would kill both her and Jamie with little or no provocation. But before she did anything, she had to ensure her brother's safety.

"Let me go to my brother," she replied. She strove to keep her voice even, but was aware that it sounded high and strained.

The man stabbed the gun in her direction. "I said drop the backpack, bitch, or I will waste you here and take it from you. Do you understand me?"

Maddie's heartbeat pounded in her ears. Jamie watched her, his face twisted with fear. She looked at him, trying to tell him without words that everything would be okay. Slowly, she slid the backpack from her shoulder and lowered it to the ground, and then raised her hands.

"Now open it and show me what's inside," the man ordered.

Dropping slowly to one knee, Maddie opened the backpack and tilted it toward the men so that they could see the cash inside.

"It's all here," she said. "Fifty thousand dollars. Now please, let me go to my brother."

He was still on his knees, weeping softly in a way that tore at Maddie's heart. She could only imagine what he'd endured.

"Take one step and I'll kill you," the man snarled. "Leave the bag where it is and back away."

Her heart nearly exploded in fear at what they might

do to Jamie. Instead of obeying, she clutched the pack in one hand. "No. You're not getting this money until I get my brother. Let me help him to the car, and then you can have the backpack."

Without warning, the man with the rifle strode over to Jamie and kicked him viciously in the ribs, knocking him onto his side. Jamie gasped for breath and tried to push himself upright, but the man kicked him again. He lay sprawled with his face in the dirt.

"No!" Maddie lurched to her feet, intent only on protecting her brother, when the first man deliberately raised his pistol, aimed it at her and pulled back the hammer.

As if time itself had slowed, she watched his face tighten with intent, even as his finger squeezed the trigger. A dark figure launched itself from the shadows beside the building, tackling the man and knocking him to the ground as a single shot rang out.

Colton.

Where had he come from? And how had he reached the building without being seen? As she stood, frozen, the second man whirled around, sweeping his weapon toward the two men as they grappled in the dirt. Almost immediately, new gunfire split the air, this time from the roof of the building, striking the man in the arm, and again in the leg. With a cry, he fell to the ground, clutching his knee, his rifle forgotten.

Maddie ran to Jamie, instinctively covering his body with her own. Peering through the haze of dust, she could just make out several shadowy figures on the roof, and more figures emerging from behind the building.

Anxiety tore through her as she shifted her attention to the two men who were locked in a death struggle just feet from where she crouched over her brother.

Colton was on his back with the other man straddling him, and Maddie caught a glimpse of the revolver that they were wrestling for control of. She watched, riveted, as they rolled over, and over again. There was a sudden, deafening gunshot, and both men went still.

_13_

MADDIE WAITED, BREATHLESS, for Colton to push the other man away and sit up, but there was no movement from either of them.

"Colton..." Hardly aware of her actions, she released Jamie, and would have rushed to Colton's side, except someone held her back. Instinctively, she struggled, lashing out at the hands that restrained her.

"Easy, Madeleine." The voice was familiar, and Maddie turned her head to see Aiden Cross, his blue eyes uncharacteristically sober.

"Aiden—"

"Stay with your brother until we make sure the area is clear."

"But Colton—"

"We'll take care of him. You stay here."

His voice brooked no argument, and slowly, Maddie became aware of the activity around her. At least a dozen other men swarmed over the area. Two were putting handcuffs on the man with the rifle, disregarding his injuries and his pleas for medical aid. Two more men were being roughly shoved out of the building in handcuffs, struggling against the men who restrained them. She recognized Siyota and several others from the reservation. At least six additional men wore distinctive black windbreakers with Police and U.S. Marshal emblazoned in yellow across the back.

"You were here the entire time," she breathed in sudden understanding. "On the roof, and hidden in those outbuildings."

"Yes, ma'am," Aiden confirmed. "Since last night, actually."

A soft groan had Maddie turning swiftly toward her brother, who had struggled to his knees beside her. One of the deputies had freed his hands, and Jamie was absently rubbing his wrists, which were chafed raw by the bindings.

"Oh, Jamie," she said, and knelt beside him, hugging him hard. "What were you thinking?"

"I'm sorry," he mumbled against her shoulder. "I'm so sorry."

"Shh. It's okay. Thank God you're safe. That's all that matters."

He pulled away enough to look at her through his good eye. "How did you manage this? Where did all these guys come from?"

Maddie gently touched his face. "I'll explain everything later. Are you okay?"

He nodded, and Maddie gave him another careful hug. "I've never been so worried in my entire life." Pulling back, she inspected the damage to his face, her heart constricting at the evidence of what he had endured. "What did they do to you?"

"Nothing I didn't deserve," he muttered. "They beat me up pretty good, but I'll survive. Thank God you came. I think they would have killed me if you hadn't brought the money."

"We'll get you to a hospital." She glanced beyond him. "Sit here for a minute, okay? Don't move. I'll be right back."

Standing up, she turned to where Colton still lay on the ground beneath the other man. Her heart was gripped in a cold fist. He should have been moving by now, should have pushed the body of the other man aside and sat up. Aiden and a U.S. marshal were crouched over the two men, and as Maddie took a tentative step toward them, they rolled the body of the top man off Colton. The kidnapper flopped lifelessly onto his back. His eyes were open, but sightless, and Maddie could see that he was dead.

Aiden bent over Colton, pressing two fingers against his throat as he checked for a pulse. Maddie felt her own throat close in fear as she dropped to her knees by his side. Colton's face was ashen, and his normally burnished skin looked waxy and pale. One of the U.S. marshals who crouched beside Aiden tore Colton's shirt open, and for the first time, Maddie saw the blood that soaked his black T-shirt and pooled in the dust beneath him.

He wore no protective vest beneath his shirt, and blood seeped in a steady stream from a small hole just above his hip bone. A wave of dizziness washed over

Maddie and she turned away, feeling weak and nauseous.

"Somebody get her out of here," the marshal growled as he applied pressure to the wound.

She turned back, shaking her head in denial. "No, please. I want to stay with him." Her voice broke as she put a hand on Colton's chest. "I need to stay with him."

The marshal looked sharply at her. "Are you Madeleine Howe?"

She nodded. The man was good-looking in a serious, law-enforcement kind of way, with his short hair and square jaw. His eyes were the color of tempered glass, and he had an air of authority that was impossible to ignore.

His lips tightened. "I'm Marshal Jason Cooper. Deputy Black works for me. If it had been up to me, I'd have had you arrested that first day. In fact, I ordered Deputy Black to bring you in, but he insisted you needed his help."

Marshal Cooper didn't actually say that it was her fault Colton had been shot, but Maddie heard the unspoken message all the same. Guilt jackknifed through her. It *was* her fault that he'd been injured. He hadn't planned on bringing her to the silver mine, and therefore hadn't planned on needing two protective vests. When he'd made the decision to bring her, he'd given her the only vest he had, leaving himself vulnerable and unprotected.

He'd taken the bullet that had been meant for her. She hadn't listened to him, and had thought she could somehow manipulate the kidnappers into releasing her brother, when she should have stuck to the plan and returned to the car. Now he lay injured, possibly even dying, because of her foolish behavior. The thought of losing him was so incredibly painful that she almost doubled over with the force of it.

"Is he going to live?" Her voice trembled, and she was helpless to prevent her tears. Reaching down, she gripped Colton's hand in hers, willing him to feel her presence. In the distance, she could hear the wail of approaching sirens.

"He's lost a lot of blood. I suspect the bullet may have nicked an artery," Marshal Cooper replied, keeping his hands pressed over the wound. "An ambulance is on the way."

Maddie's chest tightened with emotion, and she didn't trust herself to speak, so she simply nodded, her vision blurring.

"How's your brother?" the marshal asked.

Maddie glanced at Jamie, realizing she'd completely forgotten about him in her concern for Colton. She was relieved to see Siyota and another man tending to his injuries. "He's pretty busted up, but he's alive," she replied. "Thanks to you and your men."

Even as she spoke, three ambulances and two police cruisers passed through the gates, creating a cloud of dust as they drew to a stop by the entrance of the building. Two EMTs immediately began to assess Colton's condition and worked to staunch his bleeding. Stepping back to where her brother still sat on the dusty ground, Maddie knelt beside him and put her arm around him, watching as the first responders worked to save Colton's life. She had never felt so helpless.

They put an oxygen mask over his face and inserted an IV drip into one arm before they carefully transferred him to a stretcher and carried him over to a waiting ambulance. She'd never seen him look so vulnerable.

"Do you want to ride with him?" her brother asked.

Dragging her attention back to Jamie, she forced a brief smile. "No. I want to ride with you."

She helped him to his feet as two more EMTs approached to assess his injuries, and walked with him to a second waiting ambulance. But her eyes were on Colton as he lay motionless on a gurney several feet away.

Marshal Cooper drew her aside, and she had to drag her attention away from Colton in order to focus on what his colleague was saying. He carried the backpack of money, and Maddie could see it had been sealed with a zip tie, and now bore a bright yellow tag with the U.S. Marshal emblem on it.

"Your brother needs you, Ms. Howe." He spoke quietly. "He's been through a traumatic ordeal. We'll get him checked out at the hospital, but then I'll need to get some information from him about the men who took him. Aiden will ride with Colton."

"Will they take my brother to the same hospital as Colton?"

Marshal Cooper nodded. "Yes, ma'am. I also want to thank you for your actions today. Because of your help, we've apprehended three members of the notorious Canterino crime family, and eliminated a fourth. We finally have the evidence we need to indict them and begin dismantling their rackets ring."

"I had nothing to do with it," she said soberly. "You should thank Colton, Aiden and the others."

She watched as the ambulance carrying Colton pulled away, lights flashing, and her heart went with him.

She loved him.

The realization was so sudden, and so overwhelming, that for a moment her legs went wobbly.

"Ma'am, are you okay?"

Marshal Cooper watched her with an expression of concern.

"I'm fine," she assured him, but she knew she wasn't. Colton Black had worked his way into her heart. If he died, a part of her would die, too.

"Then let's get your brother to the hospital," the marshal said briskly. He handed her up into the back of the ambulance. "We'll talk later."

Maddie climbed in beside Jamie, noting that the EMTs had bandaged the worst of his injuries. Marshal Cooper closed the doors, and Maddie watched through the windows as he grew smaller in the distance until finally, the ambulance turned a corner and he disappeared from sight.

The ride to the hospital seemed to last forever, although in reality it took less than twenty minutes. Once they arrived, Jamie was swept off to the emergency room for further assessment and treatment. While he was being cared for, Maddie went in search of Colton.

She found Aiden pacing a waiting area on the second floor, his expression grim as he spoke in low tones on his cell phone. When he saw her, he ended the call and came over to take her in his arms and give her a reassuring hug.

"Hey," he said, "are you okay?"

Maddie nodded and pushed him away. "Where is he? Can I see him?"

"He's in surgery."

"How bad is he?" Maddie strove to keep her voice steady, but was unable to prevent the wobble that crept into it. "Is he going to make it?"

Aiden passed a hand over his eyes. "I don't know. I didn't really have a chance to talk to the doctors before they wheeled him into the O.R."

"Okay." Maddie drew in a deep breath, willing herself to remain calm, when all she really wanted to do was collapse in an emotional puddle on the floor. "I'll wait here with you, at least for a while."

"How is your brother?"

"He's dehydrated, and the doctors think he might have some cracked ribs, but he's going to make a full recovery. They've taken him down for X-rays, and then they're going to admit him overnight for observation. I told him I'd come to his room when I knew how Colton was doing."

"Do you want something to drink? Bottled water or maybe a cup of coffee?" Aiden asked.

"No, thanks." Maddie didn't think she could eat or drink anything right now. Her insides were churning with anxiety. She walked over to one of the small seat-ing areas, dropped into a chair and buried her face in her hands.

She sensed rather than saw Aiden come sit beside her, and didn't protest when he put an arm around her shoulders and drew her to his side. "Hey, he's going to be okay. I've known Colton my whole life, and he's pretty damned tough. He'll pull through."

Maddie nodded, wanting desperately to believe him. But the next several hours seemed interminable as she alternately waited for Colton to come out of surgery, and spent time with Jamie, who had been sedated and moved to a private room. By the time she returned to the waiting area for the third time in as many hours, Aiden had been joined by Jason Cooper, Siyota Fast Horse and Colton's mother and stepfather. They were waiting in somber silence when two men finally made their way down the corridor toward them.

Maddie surged to her feet, aware that the others did the same. One man wore the medical scrubs of a surgeon. The second wore khakis and a crisp white shirt with the sleeves rolled up. There was something vaguely familiar about him that made Maddie think they had met before, but as they drew closer, she realized they hadn't. He was an older man in his late fifties, and while he was distinguished-looking, Maddie realized she didn't know him.

"It was touch and go for a while," said the surgeon. "A fragment of the bullet was lodged near his spine, but we were able to remove it. He's going to pull through."

"Oh, thank God," Maddie breathed, her knees going

weak again. She was hardly aware of Aiden holding her up.

"I flew here as soon as Aiden called me," said the man in khakis, speaking directly to Colton's mother.

Susan Waite stepped forward and embraced him. "Thank you."

"Don't thank me. I didn't perform the surgery," the man replied. "Dr. Carroll is the one who saved his life."

"Thank you for being here," she said, stepping out of his embrace. "It means a lot to me."

"He's our son. Where else would I be?"

Maddie understood then why the man looked so familiar. He was Colton's father. He and Colton shared a tall, muscular physique, but that's where the similarity ended. Where Colton was all burnished skin and black hair and eyes, his father had light brown hair and gray eyes. But Colton had inherited the older man's dimples, as well as his manner of speech. When Colton's father spoke, you had a sense that everything would be okay.

While the surgeon provided details of the surgery, and what they could expect over the next several days, Colton's father stepped forward and extended a hand to Maddie.

"You must be Madeleine." His gray eyes were warmly assessing. "I'm Simon Black, his father."

She shook his hand. "How did you know who I was?"

"I spoke to Colton yesterday, and he talked about you in great detail." Simon grinned as Maddie's face grew warm. "And his first words in the recovery room just now were about you. He wanted to make sure you were okay."

"He's awake?" Maddie knew she had no right to see him, not when his parents and best friend were waiting to visit him, but every cell in her body ached to be near him. She needed to see him, to assure herself that he really was okay.

"He's heavily sedated," Simon was saying. "He probably won't come around for several more hours, and even then he'll be under the influence of some pretty strong drugs." He smiled. "I'd suggest you come back tomorrow, but something tells me you wouldn't listen."

Maddie felt a reluctant smile tug at her mouth. "My brother is in a room downstairs, so I'm planning on staying the night. But even if he wasn't, I couldn't leave Colton."

Reaching into his shirt pocket, Simon withdrew a small notepad and pen and scribbled on it before tearing the sheet free and handing it to her. "Here's my number. I'm staying in Reno for the next few days until Colton is released. Call me if you need anything." He glanced to where Susan and her husband were still talking with the surgeon. "I'm taking his mother and Billy out for a quick lunch. You're welcome to come with us. In fact, I'd like it very much if you'd join us."

"Thank you, but I think I'd feel more comfortable staying here," Maddie demurred.

He nodded. "I understand. I'll take Susan in to see him now, but we won't be long."

Maddie watched as Colton's mom and stepfather went with Simon. Staying behind was the hardest thing she had ever done.

"Ms. Howe?"

She turned to see Marshal Cooper eyeing her.

"Why don't I take your statement now while we're waiting?"

Needing a distraction, Maddie nodded. For the next thirty minutes, as Siyota and Aiden listened, she told the marshal everything that had transpired since she'd received the funeral wreath and note from Jamie's kidnappers. The only thing she left out were the intimate details of her time with Colton.

Marshal Cooper studied his hands. "You know," he finally said, slanting her an amused glance, "I should press charges against you."

"But you won't."

"No. Consider it a professional courtesy toward Colton." He rose to his feet and slid his notepad and pen back into his pocket. "But I would advise you to have a long discussion with your brother about the pitfalls of gambling."

Maddie smiled at him. "Don't worry. I think he got the message. He's going back to school, and any money he receives, he's going to have to work for."

Marshal Cooper arched an eyebrow, and his lips lifted in an answering smile. "Good luck with that, Ms. Howe."

CAUTIOUSLY, MADDIE ENTERED Colton's room. His parents and stepfather had left the hospital, but would return later that afternoon. Marshal Cooper, Aiden and Siyota had promised to drop by the following day to check on Colton's progress. Jamie was resting in a room just down the hallway, and for now, Maddie could visit with Colton undisturbed. But she was unprepared to see him in his condition.

He lay in the narrow hospital bed with an IV drip attached to his arm and a heart monitor hooked to one finger. His eyes were closed, and if she hadn't seen the slow rise and fall of his chest, she might have doubted that he was alive. The room smelled faintly of lemon-scented disinfectant and alcohol, and the shades on the window had been drawn, casting the room in cool shadows.

Quietly, Maddie pulled a chair up to the side of the bed and lowered the rail so she could reach out and hold his hand. He was completely unresponsive and unaware of her presence, and her heart broke a little at seeing him so helpless. She turned his hand over in her own, studying the strong fingers and short, neat nails. A faint scar bisected the pad of his thumb, and she smoothed her fingertip over it, wondering how he had acquired it.

Despite the fact that Colton had shared the story of his upbringing with her, she knew so little about him. She didn't even know what his favorite color was, although she suspected he would say it was black, like his name. She knew he liked roasted chicken with biscuits, and that he preferred to spend his spare time at his cabin, fishing. He loved his family and maintained a close relationship with his childhood friends. She knew he was honorable and decent, and that if their paths hadn't crossed at that roadside diner, there might have been a very different outcome to this whole situation.

Colton would be unharmed and probably kicking

back at his cabin with a cold beer and a fishing pole. Jamie might be injured far worse than he was.

And she would never have known what it was like to be fully alive. In fact, if not for Colton, she might be dead. He had taken a bullet that had been meant for her. Tears blurred her vision as she pressed her hand against his, palm to palm. Her own hand was smaller and slender in comparison, her skin pale against his. She had placed both her and Jamie's lives in his capable hands.

"Please be okay," she whispered fiercely through her tears, and pressed his hand against her cheek. "Because I'm falling for you, too, and I'm sorry I didn't tell you earlier."

"I already knew."

Maddie raised her head in astonishment and saw Colton watching her through half-open eyes, a weary smile lifting one corner of his mouth. With a glad cry, she flung herself against his neck, careful not to disturb his injury. She rained kisses on his cheeks, his eyes and finally his mouth before she buried her face against his shoulder, not wanting him to see her cry. He held her close with one arm, sliding his hand into her hair as he pressed his mouth against her temple.

"Shh," he murmured. "It's okay. I'm okay. I'll be out of here in a day or two."

"Oh, Colton." Her sobs were muffled against his shoulder. "You crazy man, you could have been killed."

"Not a chance," he replied. "Not when I have so much to live for."

Maddie pulled back enough to search his face, but kept one hand entwined with his. "Are you in any pain?"

"Not much. I asked the doc to hold off on any more meds until after I saw you." Colton wound a tendril of her hair around one finger and held her gaze. "I'm better now I know you're safe. How's your brother?"

"He's fine," she assured him, drinking him in. "A little banged up, but nothing serious."

"Good." Colton shifted against the pillow, and winced. Immediately, Maddie would have moved away, but he refused to release her. "No, you're fine."

"You're in pain," she protested. "Let me get a nurse to bring you something."

"Later," he insisted. "I want to talk to you first."

Maddie swiped at her damp cheeks with her free hand and nodded. "Okay. But only for a short time." She gave a small laugh. "I think your father, Aiden and Marshal Cooper would each gladly put me away for life if I let you overexert yourself."

Colton laughed and then groaned a little, but refused to release Maddie's hand when she sat up. "Where are my things? My clothes?"

She glanced quickly around the room and saw a plastic hospital bag on a chair in the corner. Releasing his hand, she retrieved the bag and carried it to the bed. "Your clothes are in here. What do you need?"

"Look in the front pocket of my jeans."

Maddie sifted through the items inside the bag, briefly lifting his bloodstained shirt and seeing the tiny tear in the fabric where the bullet had passed through. With a small shudder of distaste, she dropped the shirt and searched through the front pockets of his jeans.

"Is this what you want?" She withdrew a small key

on a chain and handed it to Colton, but he pushed it back toward her and folded her fingers around it.

"No, it's yours."

"Mine?" Maddie looked at him in bewilderment. "I've never seen this before. It must be yours."

"No. It's yours. There's something else, in the back pocket of my jeans."

"Colton, I don't think—"

"Please, Madeleine, just get it."

Maddie frowned, but searched his pockets and withdrew a folded envelope. She was about to hand it to him when she saw the writing on the outside of the envelope. There, in her grandfather's distinctive scrawl, was written one word: *Maddie*. She looked at Colton in bewilderment.

"What is this? Why do you have it?" She walked toward the window, where the light was better, casting one curious glance at Colton. He looked tired and pale, but his expression was resigned.

"I took the key from your grandfather's cabin. It was in that tin box, and you didn't care about anything except the money."

"But what about this?" she asked, feeling her chest tighten with emotion. "Why didn't I know about this letter?"

"Because it's been locked away in a safety deposit box at the U.S. Bank in Reno."

Maddie looked at him in surprise. "That's what the key was for? A safety deposit box?"

He nodded and tried to push himself to a sitting position, his expression tightening with pain.

"Colton, no," she said, returning to his side. "Please don't. You'll hurt yourself."

"I need you to know what was in that safety deposit box, Madeleine."

She sat down on the edge of the bed and took his hand in hers. "Okay, I'm listening."

"I obtained a search warrant and opened the box yesterday afternoon. It contained a little over two hundred thousand dollars in cash. And that letter."

Maddie stared at him, uncomprehending. "What?"

"Your grandfather wasn't just ranting when he said he had a fortune hidden in the cabin," Colton explained. "But the key was what he referred to, not the money."

Maddie sat back, stunned. She recalled how her grandfather had insisted the cabin was a gold mine, but she hadn't understood his meaning. She'd thought it was the dementia talking. But Colton had seen the key, and knew where it belonged.

"Why didn't you say something to me then?" she asked.

"Because I had no idea what the box would contain." He gave her a tender, tolerant look. "Besides, would you have listened?"

Maddie smiled ruefully and caressed his lean cheek with the back of her fingers. "Probably not. I'd have thought it was a trick. But that much money? How in the world—"

"Read his letter, sweetheart."

She turned the envelope over in her hands. It was still sealed. "You haven't read it."

"Of course not."

He sounded a little indignant, and Maddie gave him an apologetic smile. "Sorry."

Tearing the envelope open, she withdrew the paper inside with fingers that trembled and unfolded it. The date at the top indicated the letter had been written nearly eight years before her grandfather's death. That would have been about the same time that Jamie had run away and come to live with her, when her grandpa's drinking had been at its worst. The penmanship was crooked and messy like a child's—or like a drunk's—and Maddie wondered if he had written the letter during one of his drinking binges, and had then forgotten about it. What other reason could there be for not having given her the letter sooner?

Swallowing hard, she read it, and then read it again. By the time she was finished, she couldn't stop the tears that flowed unchecked down her face.

"Hey, come here," Colton said, and pulled her close so that her cheek was once more pressed against his shoulder. "Everything is going to be okay, I promise."

Maddie nodded and sniffed. "I know. My grandfather wrote that he's had this money for years, but guilt prevented him from ever spending it." Sitting up, she pulled a tissue from the box on the bedside table and wiped her eyes, smiling apologetically at Colton. "We don't need to talk about this now. You need to rest, and I need to let you."

But Colton's grip on her arm as she tried to stand was surprisingly strong. "Madeleine, I'm fine. I can rest later. Tell me what the letter says."

There was no mistaking the insistence in his tone.

"Okay, but you need to stop me if you feel at all tired," she said. The truth was, she wanted to tell him what was in the letter. She wanted to share everything with him.

"I'm not tired," he said, but he let her adjust the pillows behind his shoulders to a more comfortable position.

"My grandfather gambled his entire life," she began, "and he was pretty good at it. But when my father showed signs of becoming a compulsive gambler, Grandpa tried to counsel him, telling him he was going to lose everything, including his kids."

Colton reached out and took her hand in his, squeezing her fingers in sympathy.

"Eventually," Maddie continued, "my dad did lose everything, including money that wasn't his to lose. My grandfather refused to bail him out, thinking he was teaching him a valuable lesson. But he never guessed that my father would commit suicide."

Colton made a sound of sympathy. "I'm so sorry, sweetheart."

Maddie cleared her throat against the lump that had formed there. "My grandfather had the money to help him, and I don't think he ever forgave himself for not giving it to my dad. That's what drove him to drink so heavily."

"That would be a heavy burden for anyone to bear."

"My mother had passed away the year before from cancer, and my grandfather ended up with custody of me and my brother." She traced a finger over the letter. "He writes here that the day we moved in with him was the day he stopped gambling. He wanted to be a good role model, and he intended to use the money he had to raise us. But he couldn't stop himself from drinking."

"He did the best that he could," Colton said quietly.

Maddie nodded. "Yes. He closes the letter by asking for our forgiveness, saying that he hopes the money he's left us will somehow compensate for the mess he and my father made of our lives."

Colton tugged her down until she was lying beside him on the narrow bed, with her head under his chin. "I'm so sorry you had to go through that," he said. "But I'll never be sorry about what happened these past few days."

"Me, neither," Maddie agreed. "Except for you being shot, that is."

"What will you do now?" he asked. "Two hundred thousand dollars is a lot of money."

She wanted to tell him that she didn't care about the money; she just wanted to be with him. She'd gotten by her entire life without having much money, and she didn't need it in order to be happy.

"I don't know," she said, smiling. "I'll probably just keep it in reserve for the next time I need to ransom my brother."

Colton arched an eyebrow in a look she'd come to know very well over the past few days. "I'm not sure I like the sound of that."

"No," she agreed. "I'm not going to let that happen. I'll start by getting myself a new car. And Jamie has agreed to get some help for his gambling addiction. Maybe I could use the money to help other teens who have addictions—kids who might not have access to treatment. Jamie's also going to do an outreach program, to warn other kids about the perils of gambling. That was his idea."

"Hey, look at me," Colton said softly.

Maddie raised her head and found herself trapped in his black gaze.

"I think all of that's a fine idea," he said, "so long as it doesn't exclude me."

"Does that mean you're still interested in me?" she asked, suddenly shy.

Colton chuckled. "Oh, yeah. In fact, I don't think I'll be letting you out of my sight anytime soon. I'm still on vacation, and I thought maybe once we get Jamie settled, you might consider spending the next week or so with me at my cabin."

"I don't know," she hedged, pretending to consider. "I'm not much good at fishing."

"I can show you everything you need to know," he assured her with a grin, "but something tells me we won't be doing much fishing."

"I like the sound of that," she replied. "In fact, I think you'll need to give me a new Shoshone name, because my days of running are over." She leaned forward to kiss him, taking care not to disturb his wound.

"I'm not fragile," he growled, and wrapped an arm around her and pulled her more fully across his chest. "And I've been dying to kiss you since you came into this room. Tell me again."

"Tell you what?" she asked, breathless.

"That you're falling for me."

Maddie laughed softly. "Past tense, Colton. I've fallen for you, hard, and there's no way I'm letting you out of my sight."

"Sounds like a pair of handcuffs might be in order," he said. "Just out of curiosity, how attached are you to Elko? Have you ever considered coming out to California? I hear they're in desperate need of some good accountants."

Maddie stared at him. "You're not kidding."

"Nope. Your brother is at Caltech in Pasadena, which is just a couple of hours from where I live in San Diego. Wouldn't you like to be closer to him?"

"I'd like to be closer to you," she admitted.

"Then come and stay with me," he urged softly. "See if you like the area, and then we can talk about living arrangements. I have a nice place near the water, but I'd understand if you want your own place. You'd have no trouble finding work. Like I said, there's always a need for certified public accountants."

"I'd like that," she said, too overwhelmed to say more.

"Hey, you okay?"

"Yes," she assured him, smiling.

"Then come closer," he said, just before he drew her down and covered her mouth with his.

Maddie leaned into the kiss, happier than she could ever recall being. Jamie would recover. She wasn't going to be arrested, nor lose her job. Her immediate financial worries were a thing of the past, and she had the means to help others who struggled with addiction issues. But most important, Colton was alive, and he wanted to be with her.

Neither of them noticed when the door opened and two nurses peeked in. The women sighed in delight at the sight of Maddie being passionately kissed by the handsome U.S. marshal, and then quietly closed the door.

* * * * *

#787 CAPTIVATE ME
Unrated!
by Kira Sinclair
What is it about Mardi Gras that makes everyone lose their mind? When Alyssa Vaughn notices a masked stranger watching her undress through her bedroom window, the Bacchus attitude takes over. But wait until she finds out who he is!

#788 TEXAS OUTLAWS: COLE
The Texas Outlaws
by Kimberly Raye
Cole Chisholm's love life is even wilder than the horses he rides. When Nikki Barbie asks him to pretend to be her boyfriend, he agrees...but only if some wild, wicked nights are included!

#789 ALONE WITH YOU
Made in Montana
by Debbi Rawlins
Alexis Worthington is smart, ambitious and has a wild streak that alienated her from her family. Now's her chance to prove herself to them. But working with rodeo rider Will Tanner—she's finding it difficult to behave!

#790 UNEXPECTED TEMPTATION
The Berringers
by Samantha Hunter
Luke Berringer thinks he's finally put his past to rest when he catches the woman who ruined his life—but in Vanessa Grant has he actually found the woman who will heal his heart?

REQUEST YOUR FREE BOOKS!
2 FREE NOVELS PLUS 2 FREE GIFTS!

HARLEQUIN
Blaze®
red-hot reads!

YES! Please send me 2 FREE Harlequin® Blaze™ novels and my 2 FREE gifts (gifts are worth about $10). After receiving them, if I don't wish to receive any more books, I can return the shipping statement marked "cancel." If I don't cancel, I will receive 4 brand-new novels every month and be billed just $4.74 per book in the U.S. or $4.96 per book in Canada. That's a savings of at least 14% off the cover price. It's quite a bargain. Shipping and handling is just 50¢ per book in the U.S. and 75¢ per book in Canada.* I understand that accepting the 2 free books and gifts places me under no obligation to buy anything. I can always return a shipment and cancel at any time. Even if I never buy another book, the two free books and gifts are mine to keep forever.

150/350 HDN F4WC

Name _____ (PLEASE PRINT) _____

Address _____ Apt. # _____

City _____ State/Prov. _____ Zip/Postal Code _____

Signature (if under 18, a parent or guardian must sign)

Mail to the Harlequin® Reader Service:
IN U.S.A.: P.O. Box 1867, Buffalo, NY 14240-1867
IN CANADA: P.O. Box 609, Fort Erie, Ontario L2A 5X3

Want to try two free books from another line?
Call 1-800-873-8635 or visit www.ReaderService.com.

* Terms and prices subject to change without notice. Prices do not include applicable taxes. Sales tax applicable in N.Y. Canadian residents will be charged applicable taxes. Offer not valid in Quebec. This offer is limited to one order per household. Not valid for current subscribers to Harlequin Blaze books. All orders subject to credit approval. Credit or debit balances in a customer's account(s) may be offset by any other outstanding balance owed by or to the customer. Please allow 4 to 6 weeks for delivery. Offer available while quantities last.

Your Privacy—The Harlequin® Reader Service is committed to protecting your privacy. Our Privacy Policy is available online at www.ReaderService.com or upon request from the Harlequin Reader Service.

We make a portion of our mailing list available to reputable third parties that offer products we believe may interest you. If you prefer that we not exchange your name with third parties, or if you wish to clarify or modify your communication preferences, please visit us at www.ReaderService.com/consumerchoice or write to us at Harlequin Reader Service Preference Service, P.O. Box 9062, Buffalo, NY 14269. Include your complete name and address.

HB13R2

Captivate Me

by Kira Sinclair, coming March 2014 from
Harlequin Blaze.

Amid the revelry of Mardi Gras, Beckett Kayne just wanted a
moment of peace. He was enjoying the solitude when a light
snapped on in the apartment across the alley.

She stood, framed by the window. A soft radiance lit her
from behind, painting her in an ethereal splash of color that
made her seem dreamy and tragic and somehow unreal.

Maybe that was why he kept watching. Logically, he realized he was intruding, but there was something about her....

Her eyelids slid closed and her head tipped back. Exhaustion was stamped into every line of her body, but that didn't
detract from her allure. In fact, it made Beckett want to reach
out and hold her. To take her weight and the exhaustion on
himself.

Her hands drifted slowly up her body, settling at the top
button of her blouse. With sure fingers, she popped it open.
And another. And another. The edge of her red-hot bra came
into view revealing an enticing swell of skin.

Tension snapped through Beckett's body. The hedonistic pressure of the night must have gotten to him, after all. Because, even as his brain was screaming at him to give her privacy, he couldn't do it.

It had been a very long time since any woman had pulled this kind of immediate physical reaction from him.

Perhaps it was the air of innocence not even the windowpane and ten feet of alley could camouflage. She was simply herself—unconsciously sensual.

Shifting, Beckett dropped his foot and settled his waist against the edge of the balcony railing. He wanted to be the one uncovering her soft skin. Running his fingers over her body. Hearing the hitch of her breath when he discovered a sensitive spot.

Maybe it was his movement that caught her attention. Suddenly her head snapped sideways and she looked straight into his eyes.

Her fingers stilled. Surprise, embarrassment and anger flitted across her face before finally settling into something darker and a hell of a lot more sinful.

Her arms stretched wide. She undulated, rolling her hips and ribs and spine in a way that begged him to touch.

And then the blinds snapped down between them.

Pick up CAPTIVATE ME by Kira Sinclair, available in March 2014 wherever you buy Harlequin® Blaze® books.

Get ready for a wild ride!

Cole Chisholm's love life is even wilder than the horses he rides. When Nikki Barbie asks him to pretend to be her boyfriend, he agrees...but only if some wild, wicked nights are included.

Pick up the final chapter of
The Texas Outlaws miniseries

Texas Outlaws: Cole

by *USA TODAY* bestselling author

Kimberly Raye

AVAILABLE FEBRUARY 18, 2014,
wherever you buy Harlequin Blaze books.

HARLEQUIN®

Blaze®

Red-Hot Reads
www.Harlequin.com

HB79792

Rules are made to be broken!

Alexis Worthington is smart, ambitious and has a wild streak that alienated her from her family. Now's her chance to prove herself to them. But working with rodeo rider Will Tanner—she's finding it difficult to behave!

Don't miss

Alone with You

by reader-favorite author

Debbi Rawlins

AVAILABLE FEBRUARY 18, 2014, wherever you buy Harlequin Blaze books.